Trick of the Heart

ALSO BY MAEVE BUCHANAN

Contemporary Romance

The Thurston Hotel Series:

The Starlight Garden, Book 7

Trick of the Heart

A WOMEN OF STAMPEDE NOVEL

MAEVE BUCHANAN

Best wishes!

Maeve Buchanan

Published 2018 by Maeve Buchanan

ISBN: 978-0-9953014-2-9 (Print edition)

Design and cover art by Su Kopil, Earthly Charms
Copyediting by Ted Williams

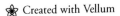 Created with Vellum

DEDICATION

For Dawn and Doug

FOREWORD

It's a pleasure to introduce Maeve Buchanan's second work of romantic fiction. Trick of the Heart ushers the reader into the rodeo arena, a place where one trick rider struggles with fear and past trauma, while the other, a Cossack rider, champions a woman's spirit while awakening her feminine desires.

A certain enchantment exists between Jaycee and Sergei. From the first dance to the last kiss, Maeve fills the romance with sweetness, intrigue and breath-taking inspiration. At times, the author had me whispering her narrative, speaking with a Russian accent.

See for yourself, *zvyozdochka. My little star...*

Shelley Kassian, author of The Half Mile of Baby Blue. Book two in the Women of Stampede series.

PREFACE

Hello and welcome to Trick of the Heart, the seventh book in the Women of Stampede series!

This project is very close to my heart. I grew up in the town of Okotoks, just south of Calgary, surrounded by townsfolk, farmers, ranchers and rodeo people. I'm so grateful to my parents that they decided to move West and settle in one of the prettiest and most interesting towns in Alberta.

One of the highlights of our year was going to rodeos in the spring and summer. From the Little Britches in High River, Alberta, to the Calgary Stampede, we couldn't wait to soak up the rodeo atmosphere. For many years, my dad enjoyed calf roping and I remember getting together with other families around Okotoks to visit and practice roping.

As a young girl, I watched in awe and amazement as the Flying Duces, Jerri and Joy Duce, performed their trick riding act at various rodeos in Alberta. At that age, I could imagine no more exciting or glamorous career than being a trick rider.

Well, I didn't become a trick rider but as you see I did become a writer! These early memories are strongly imprinted and I wanted to share some of my excitement about rodeo life with my readers.

In particular, I want to pay tribute to all the cowgirls who have shown their talent, grit and determination while upholding the tradition of the rodeo. They are the real Women of Stampede.

ACKNOWLEDGMENTS

I am deeply indebted to Shelley Kassian and Katie O'Connor, who initiated this wonderful Western series. I'm so glad I was asked to be part of it!

Shelley mentored and supported me through all the stages of writing, editing and preparing for publication, and worked diligently to help me shape and refine my story. I cannot thank her enough for her professionalism and friendship.

A big thank you to author Katie O'Connor, team lead for the Women of Stampede series. Your consistent encouragement and support, and your organization of all the details for the series played an essential part in the creation of this book.

Sincere thanks to my beta readers and content editors, Shelley Kassian and Alyssa Palmer, whose edits and suggestions made this a much better book. Thanks also to Ted Williams, who made an indispensable contribution as copy editor. Credit for my beautiful cover design goes to Su Kopil of Earthly Charms Graphic Design.

Many thanks to Doug Milligan, who assisted me with details pertaining to the Calgary Stampede and rodeo in general.

Thank you to Yuliia Malanych, who helped me with the Russian language aspects of the manuscript. *Spasebo*!

My gratitude and thanks to Cindy Spears, who checked in almost every day to see how I was doing and encouraged me on those days when the task seemed endless. Yours is truly a gift of the heart.

No author can fail to be grateful for the support and encouragement of family and friends during the development of a creative project. I have been deeply blessed in that regard. To my wonderful family and many close friends, thank you for your love and faith in me.

To my readers: thank you for reading this book! I write because of you, and I welcome your feedback and ideas. Please visit me at my website and on social media so we can get to know each other.

Enjoy your adventures with the Women of Stampede!

Love, Maeve

CHAPTER 1

*S*he had to get this right. *She had to.*

Jaycee's hands trembled as she tightened the cinch. What was wrong with her? Here she was, an experienced horsewoman since the age of three, scared to death to even tack up her horse.

Luna puffed out her belly as Jaycee gave another yank on the cinch.

"Luna, behave!" Jaycee warned, smacking the horse's side. One of Luna's ears flicked back. "No cheating!" Luna relaxed as Jaycee tightened the cinch and tested the saddle with both hands.

"That should do it."

The specially designed trick saddle had been her mother's and now it was hers. Tried and true.

Yet she was afraid. So afraid.

Don't think about it. Just do it.

She swung up into the saddle and urged Luna into a slow canter around the paddock. It was a gorgeous morning, perfect conditions. The paddock was dry and hard packed. Luna's movements were smooth and rhythmic. For the hundredth time, Jaycee thanked her stars that she had found this horse. They were a perfect team, each trusting the other to the point where they could anticipate each other's moves. Jaycee knew she had to try and suppress the fear she had been feeling, or Luna would notice it. She urged Luna into a smooth gallop. Taking a few deep breaths, Jaycee swung her leg over the saddle and started with a Front Fender, followed by a Back Bend. She then went into a full Stroud Layout, arms spread wide. Next, a few Touchdowns. Finally, she stood and went into the Hippodrome Stance. Warmed up, she lowered herself back down into the saddle.

Now, Jaycee. Heart pounding, she tried to relax and trust her body memory, listening to the sound of the hoof beats and Luna's steady breathing. Her anxiety grew as she prepared to execute the Death Drag. Anxiety suddenly went to terror as images of the past rose in her mind. She took a few more deep breaths and tried to control her thoughts.

You can do this. Jaycee, you know you can do this. You've done it hundreds of times.

NOW, Jaycee. NOW. NOW. NOW.

The moment passed, Jaycee stayed upright in the saddle and Luna galloped on.

Oh God, what's wrong with me?

Tears ran down her cheeks, drying quickly in the wind. She reined Luna to a trot and headed back to the gate, where her father, Ellis McRae, was leaning over the fence. He didn't say a word, but quietly opened the gate and let her ride through. She dismounted and led her horse back to the barn.

Maybe tomorrow. I'll keep trying.

Later, in the ranch house, her mother, Ruth, spooned some stew onto her plate for lunch, and her father handed her a platter of sliced homemade bread.

"Looks like it'll be another fine day tomorrow," Ellis said, glancing up at her mother. "I might try to get that fence fixed over near the shed."

Her mother nodded absentmindedly, and sat down to eat.

"I'll give you a hand, Dad," Jaycee offered.

"Thanks, darlin', that would be fine," Ellis said, buttering a piece of bread before dunking it in his stew.

~

THAT AFTERNOON AROUND FOUR, Jaycee parked her truck in front of the Home Ground Coffee and Roasting House on Railway Street in Okotoks. Finding an empty table, she ordered a black coffee and a cinnamon roll. She sipped the coffee slowly, savoring the full taste, then cut the roll into sections. Minutes later she was joined by Megan Burns, her best friend. Megan's parents had died in a car crash a few years before and Megan, an only child, had been left alone. The McRaes had informally adopted her, since Megan and Jaycee had been inseparable pals all through their school years.

"Hey, Jaycee, how are things?" Megan waved to the waitress behind the counter, who brought over another cup. "Getting ready for Stampede?"

Jaycee concentrated on her cinnamon bun. She didn't want to talk about this, but how could she avoid it?

"Yeah, I guess. I had Luna out this morning."

"Good girl. I've made some excellent times this week with Monkey."

Megan was a barrel racer whose horse, Monkeyshines, was one of the best on the circuit. Megan had high hopes for the Stampede this year. "I think we might qualify for the National Finals in Edmonton."

"I'm sure you will. You were pretty close last year." Jaycee agreed.

"We'll see, we'll see." Megan took another long sip of her coffee. "Say, I hear Cody's back," she said, watching Jaycee closely for her reaction.

This was old news to Jaycee. Everyone in town had been telling her.

"Yeah, I heard," she said, fiddling with the sugar bowl.

"And?" Megan asked.

"I'll be glad to see him, of course."

"I hear he's been asking about you."

"I'm sure we'll cross paths. I've just been focusing on other things." Jaycee took another sip of her coffee.

Her parents and friends had always assumed that she and Cody would end up together. Cody had been her high school sweetheart, and the two had been inseparable until Cody had enrolled at the University of Alberta to do a degree in agriculture. Gradually, they had grown apart and had started dating other people. Now Cody was home for good and making plans.

While Cody was away she and her sister, Kerrie, had worked the ranch with their parents, spending every summer on the rodeo circuit with their trick riding act. They'd been trick riding since they were twelve and fourteen years old. Preparing for the circuit meant spending weekends practicing with their mother or at their trainer's place, working on building a good routine while learning the fine art of entertaining a crowd. At first, their mother had sewn their costumes. Later, they had found an affordable dressmaker in town who kept their size information and understood the importance of designing costumes that were flashy and colorful yet safe to perform in.

Jaycee's mind came back to the present. Stampede was only a couple of weeks away. Without Kerrie, she felt alone. And scared. She had to get her nerve back soon if she was going to perform effectively in front of the large grandstand crowds.

Megan frowned and reached across to hold Jaycee's hand. Jaycee realized her face had betrayed her.

"I know it's been tough, Jaycee. But it's been a year. You're still riding. That alone takes a lot of courage."

Jaycee's fingers tightened around Megan's and her eyes began to fill with tears. "I don't know, Megan, I just don't know if I can do it this year," she said.

"You can. I promise. I'm with you, girl."

Jaycee nodded and wiped the back of her hand across her eyes.

THAT EVENING, Jaycee was in the kitchen helping her mother prepare supper. Ruth sat at the table peeling potatoes while Jaycee cut up celery, cucumber and tomatoes on the kitchen counter.

"Cody's home, honey, did you know?" Ruth said.

"So I hear." Jaycee opened the fridge and pulled out some Romaine lettuce, which she began tearing into small pieces into a wooden salad bowl. "It will be nice to see him again."

"Just nice?" Ruth inquired.

"It's been a long time, Mom," Jaycee answered. "I haven't seen him since…" She stopped and then continued. "I texted back and forth with him a couple of times last year, but that's it. He was busy, I think."

"I don't doubt it," Ruth replied. "Cody's a pretty hard-working guy. The whole point of getting his degree was so he could come back and manage the Phillips' ranch. Specializing in cattle husbandry will help him build and maintain the herd his dad left him." She glanced over at her daughter. "You two were quite a pair in the old days. Always up to something!"

Jaycee laughed. "That's for sure. Remember when Cody, Kerrie and I piled up those bales of hay on the principal's desk one night after basketball practice? We were on detention in separate rooms for two weeks!"

Ruth smiled. "You kids put some of these gray hairs on my head!"

You kids. Jaycee suddenly felt the familiar pain in her chest.

"Jaycee, honey, hand me that pot."

Jaycee picked up a pot by the sink and handed it to her mother.

Ruth began putting the peeled potatoes in it. The two women were silent for a few minutes as they continued their work.

"I miss her, too," Ruth said simply. Jaycee looked up at her mother and their eyes met in mutual understanding.

They heard Ellis stamping his feet on the back porch, and the water running in the porch sink as he washed up from his chores.

Half an hour later the three of them were sitting around the table, helping themselves to tender roast beef, potatoes, corn, salad and sliced bread. Ruth had brought out a large pitcher of cold creamy milk. They ate quietly. Jaycee helped her mother clear the table and carry cups of steaming black coffee from the kitchen. Her father loved pie, and Ruth had made his favorite: rhubarb. After dessert, Ellis pushed out his chair and leaned back, placing a toothpick in his mouth.

"I saw Megan today," Jaycee offered.

"Oh yes? How's the barrel racing going?" Ellis loved to hear about Megan's rodeo ambitions.

"She's doing well," Jaycee remarked. "Monkey is making faster times, according to her."

"Those two are a good team," Ellis said. "Doesn't matter what you do, you need good teamwork between a rider and a horse."

Jaycee nodded in agreement, hoping her father wouldn't talk about what he had witnessed in the paddock that day. He glanced at her, but didn't comment.

Ruth went and fetched her knitting from the living room and sat down at the table with it.

She took a few sips of her coffee and talked as she knit.

"Ellis, Cody Phillips is home. We should invite him over for supper."

"Good idea," Ellis said. "We can all catch up."

"He was over earlier, delivering some eggs and cream from his Aunt Perdie's place," Ruth continued. "Perdie tells me he's just bought a quarter section near the river."

"He'll have his work cut out, with chores at home and fencing that property as well," Ellis remarked. "I'll go over to see if I can give him a hand."

Jaycee said nothing. She was looking forward to seeing Cody, but a bit nervous about it as well. She just hoped his visit wouldn't bring up unreasonable expectations that she and Cody would pick up where they had left off after high school.

CHAPTER 2

*S*ergei's hands moved smoothly over his horse's back, the brush in his right, the curry comb in his left. He liked this daily ritual, and so did Pasha, who stood relaxed, his tail flicking occasionally.

The Volkov Cossack Troupe had arrived in Calgary a week ago and had been assigned five stalls in one of the Stampede barns. The entire troupe, except for Sergei, had been billeted at the Fairfield Inn. Sergei preferred to rent an RV and stay in the small parking lot above the Stampede grounds. He enjoyed the solitude this arrangement provided, and it allowed him to be near the horse barns in case a problem arose with the horses.

It had been a long process to obtain the necessary paperwork to bring six people, plus five horses from Russia. As always, Sergei had been in charge of organizing the travel arrangements, making sure everyone had up-to-date passports, having the horses vetted on both sides of the Atlantic, booking the hotel, and doing detailed inventories of the tack and other equipment needed over the two weeks they would be in Canada.

In addition to these responsibilities, Sergei had faithfully adhered to an intense training schedule prior to the trip. He was exhausted and jet-lagged, but knew that he had to get himself in top condition prior to the performances, otherwise his safety would be compromised. A few days' rest and he would be fine.

This was a whole new venture for the Volkovs. They had seldom performed outside Russia, but the government had approved this visit to Canada as part of a cultural exchange with the Canadian government. Several Canadian trick riders were now in Russia, performing at one of the summer festivals in Moscow. The Volkov troupe were expected to impress the Canadians and represent their country in a diplomatic manner, but Sergei knew he might have a hard time keeping some of the troupe members from indulging in activities unsuitable for cultural ambassadors. His younger brothers, Mikhail and Dmitri, could be a little rebellious at times, but in the end, they always obeyed Sergei and his father, Petr Volkov.

Irina Petrov, the only woman in their midst, was a different story. She would definitely pose a problem when it came to controlling her behavior. Headstrong, defiant and fearless, she had shown herself capable of acting on impulse without regard for the consequences. She also had a way of leading others into trouble. Sergei didn't know quite what to do with her. He had to admit he found Irina attractive, very attractive. He had restrained himself because it wasn't right to have an affair with an employee. Still, he sometimes wondered what might happen between them if he allowed it.

The other performer that concerned him was Vladimir Ivanovich. Irina and Vladimir had both been hired only a week before the trip to Canada. Sergei had argued with Petr about this last-minute decision, but his father had been unmovable. Vladimir in particular struck Sergei as arrogant and untrustworthy.

Last week, on the plane, Irina had slid into the seat next to him and immediately ordered a double vodka 'to start the trip off right'. Before long she had her hand on his arm, leaning over him to look out the window and pushing her body close to his.

"Sergei?"

"Yes?"

"Have you ever thought about staying in Canada?"

"What do you mean?"

Irina put her lips beside his ear. "Leaving Russia for good. Defecting."

"Irina, hold your tongue!" Sergei whispered, considering the nearby passengers. "It is not wise to talk of such things in a public place! And remember, you must be very careful what you say when we get to customs."

"I do not care, Seryozha. I dream of starting a new life, in a country where I can make my own rules."

She put her lips to his ear again. "Russia is behind the times. Canada has opportunities. We could start our own troupe. Think of it! The money would pour in. Enough for a big house, a fast car and…"

"That's enough, Irina." Sergei shook his head. "We'll talk about this later."

Irina pouted and waved to the attendant for another vodka. "You'll see. Once we get to Canada, you won't want to go back."

Sergei wondered if this was true. He had been looking forward to exploring opportunities in a new country. He loved his homeland, but there was little to hold him there. His father and younger brothers were certainly capable of managing of the troupe between them. He had been thinking about starting his own riding school. He had said nothing to his father, but had given much thought to how he could make it happen.

Irina settled down in her seat, feigning sleep so she could drop her head onto his shoulder.

His father walked up from a few seats behind and took the empty aisle seat next to Irina.

"*Only three more hours before we land in Toronto,*" Petr Volkov said, quietly. "*Is everything ready?*"

Sergei nodded. "*I'll check on the horses and you and the troupe connect to the next flight. I'll follow you and meet you at the gate.*"

"*And in Calgary, the horse trailer is waiting?*"

"*Yes, Papa, it will be waiting. I'll unload the horses while you see to the luggage. I've rented a van for Dmitri to drive everyone into the city. I rented my RV at the same place.*"

"*Good.*" Sergei's father glanced down at Irina's sleeping face. "*Vodka?*"

"*Yes, she's had several,*" Sergei answered. His father chuckled.

"*This one, she has the gypsy heart. Not easy to control, but lots of passion!*" He looked at his son. "*You could do worse.*"

"*I need to stay professional, Papa. I am her boss.*"

"*Think about it, my son. She works hard, she is a good rider, and a beautiful woman. Like your mother.*" He sighed.

"*There will never be anyone like Mama,*" Sergei replied. "*Irina may be a good rider, but she hasn't got the discipline or the heart that Mama had.*" He sincerely hoped Irina was sleeping and couldn't hear this conversation. He suspected otherwise.

"*Maybe not, but a man needs a woman who understands his work.*"

"*Perhaps,*" Sergei said reluctantly.

"*Do not fall in love with some American woman, that is all I ask.*" His father frowned. "*You want a good Russian woman, who works hard and will bear healthy children.*" Sergei had heard this advice from his father since his teenage years.

"*Yes, Papa,*" he said, knowing it was useless to argue.

"Good!" Petr waved to the attendant. *"We will drink on it! Two vodkas!"*

"SERGEI! COME! TIME TO PRACTICE!"

Sergei put down the halter he was repairing to find his father and brother, Dmitri, standing outside the barn. Dmitri had his horse, Vadesh, tacked up and ready to go. As Sergei got Pasha ready, Petr took the opportunity for a little coaching.

"Remember, Dmitri, keep track of where Sergei is as he rides behind you. Use your ears. Sergei, do not follow too close behind and spook Vadesh. When you come up behind, be ready to loop your reins as you transfer across. It has to be smooth. Do not break Vadesh's pace."

"Yes, Papa." Sergei patted Pasha on the neck and then gently slid the bridle over his head.

"Yes, Papa." Dmitri gave a final check to his saddle and swung up on Vadesh.

Soon, both were urging their horses into a gallop around the paddock, Sergei following Dmitri. After three rounds, Sergei moved Pasha up alongside Vadesh. Soon the two horses were running side by side.

Sergei carefully secured his reins before focusing his attention on Vadesh and Dmitri less than two feet away. Within moments, he had grasped the strap on Vadesh's saddle and swung across until he was positioned behind his brother. Pasha, who was well-trained in this maneuver, veered away and trotted to a stop in the far corner. Dmitri secured his reins. In one smooth movement, Dmitri's feet slipped under straps on the front of the saddle and he stood up in the Hippodrome Stance. Sergei followed his lead until both men were standing upright with their arms outspread, leaning slightly forward. Vadesh galloped steadily on. After a few minutes,

Sergei and Dmitri moved back down into the saddle in reverse order, and once again stretched out their arms.

"Good work!" Petr had a wide smile on his face as they galloped past. "Sergei, Touchdowns right to left!"

Dmitri picked up his reins and kept Vadesh moving smoothly. Sergei looped his hands into the back of the saddle and began to vault, first to the right flank of the horse, touching down briefly before vaulting up and touching down on the left side. He repeated this several times.

He then flipped around until he was facing the horse's tail, bent forward and brought himself into a shoulder stand, his legs straight, boots pointed upward. After a few seconds, each move was once again reversed until he was sitting upright behind his brother, facing forward.

Dmitri took Vadesh into a trot and they headed back to where their father was standing behind the fence.

"Good." Petr then led his own horse, Mishka, into the paddock.

Sergei watched as his father executed his repertoire of stunts at a full gallop. He could never get over how skilled a horseman Petr was, even in his sixties.

One of his earliest memories was being lifted into the saddle at age three by his father. Sergei remembered being completely unafraid as his father walked him around the paddock. His mother had stood watching them with complete confidence in her husband and son.

Like Petr, she had been an exceptional rider. Marina and Petr Volkov had performed at equine exhibitions all over the world before settling down to raise their three boys. Sergei and his brothers had begun doing simple stunts by age five. Horses were a part of the family, siblings for the three little boys. Falls, bumps and bruises were common occurrences as they perfected their riding skills. That was part of learning. "You fall enough, you get sick of it," Petr said. "Then you stop falling."

He had been right.

CHAPTER 3

*J*aycee watched through the living room window as Cody Phillips parked his truck in the yard of the McRae ranch house. Not wanting to be seen, she quickly turned and took a seat on the sofa.

"Come in, Cody dear! It's so good to see you again," she heard her mother say. Ruth held the door wide open as Cody stepped inside. "Ellis and Jaycee are in the living room."

Cody hung his cowboy hat and jean jacket on the coat rack near the door. "Hello, Mrs. McRae. Good to see you, too. I'm so sorry about—"

Ruth interrupted him. "Make yourself at home," she said. "I'll just head back to the kitchen. Dinner's almost ready."

Ellis and Jaycee both stood as Cody came into the living room. Smiling, Ellis took the young man's right hand and shook it firmly. "Welcome home, son! We've missed you."

Jaycee hesitated a second and then moved forward to give Cody a quick hug. "Welcome back, Cody. Beer?"

"I could drink a beer," Cody responded with a grin. Jaycee brought three beers from the kitchen and they all sat down.

Ellis leaned toward his guest. "So tell me, how are things going over at your ranch? I was telling Ruth and Jaycee that I planned to drop over to offer some help."

"That would be great," Cody said. "I could use some help with fencing if you have time."

"Sure, no problem, what day works for you?" Ellis replied.

"Tuesday would work best," Cody said. "If that's agreeable."

"Fine. To Cody's ranch," Ellis said, lifting his bottle of beer.

"Cody's ranch," Jaycee said, clinking her bottle against theirs.

Cody smiled, pleased at the toast. "You look good, Jaycee. How's the trick riding?"

"Fine, thanks," Jaycee answered, not wanting to talk about her problems. She was grateful when Cody turned to Ellis and began outlining his plans to improve his ranch. Jaycee listened, sipping her beer and thinking how good Cody looked. His curly brown hair had been trimmed short, and he had a deep tan from working outside. His brown eyes gleamed with enthusiasm as he talked about his plans, speaking with a maturity that was new to Jaycee. Cody had changed physically, as well. His arm muscles pressed against the fabric of his shirt, and his tight Wranglers revealed strong thighs. She remembered how close they had been in the past. In those days they thought they were in love, but so much had changed. *He's not the boy I knew in high school*, she thought as she admired this new Cody.

Cody turned to Ellis. "I may be buying some more Herefords this year. I'll be going to the AltaLink Hall at the Stampede to meet some of the breeders."

Ellis leaned forward and set his empty beer bottle on the coffee table. "I remember your dad always favored Herefords. I can see why you want to stay with them. It's good you're building on what he started."

Ruth came in, wiping her hands on her yellow flowered apron. "Supper's ready, everyone!"

They made their way to the kitchen and sat at the table. It was covered in a red gingham vinyl cloth and set with white dishes and cutlery on red placemats. Straw trivets held steaming bowls of mashed potatoes, carrots, peas, and a plate of breaded pork chops. In the center of the table, a Lazy Susan held salt, pepper, butter, ketchup, and applesauce. At one end was a large bowl of green salad with tongs set in it.

"Let's say grace," Ruth suggested. "Cody?" They bowed their heads as Cody prayed briefly over the food.

"Dig in!" Ellis grinned as he forked pork chops onto each person's plate. Ruth had brought in a large jug of milk, and one of water. For a few minutes, everyone concentrated on the food.

"This is delicious, Mrs. McRae," Cody observed with enthusiasm. "I miss eating this kind of home-cooked meal since my mom passed. Dad was a great farmer, but not much of a cook."

"Thank you, Cody," Ruth said. "I guess you'll be wanting to settle down and find your own wife soon." She glanced at Jaycee.

Don't, Jaycee thought, feeling embarrassed. *Don't go there, Mom, please.*

Cody didn't take the bait.

"Maybe, one day," he said, not looking up. "Pass the potatoes, please."

After dinner, Ellis and Cody discussed the current farming reports as Jaycee helped her mother clear the table. The two women brought out coffee and blueberry pie for dessert.

Cody looked at Jaycee. "I was thinking Jaycee might like to go for a walk after supper."

"Sure, Cody," Jaycee answered. "It would be a good chance to catch up."

Stepping out into the cool, dark night, Cody and Jaycee walked along the fence, past the barn and through the meadow to a small stream they had often fished in as children.

"Beautiful night," Cody said.

"It is," Jaycee answered.

They sat on a log they had placed there years ago.

"You really have come a long way, Cody. I'm proud of you," Jaycee said, turning to him.

"Thanks, Jaycee. It was a long haul getting through university and my agricultural internship, but it was worth it. I know exactly what I'm going to do now."

Cody laid his hand on hers. "We had some good times, didn't we, you and me? Jaycee, I want you to know how sorry I am about what happened last year. I tried to tell your mom I was sorry, but she cut me off."

Jaycee swallowed. "Dad, Mom, and I are all still pretty fragile when it comes to that. Don't worry about it, Cody."

"Okay." Cody took her hand in his. "I've missed you, Jaycee."

Jaycee looked at him. "I've missed you, too, Cody."

"Would it be all right if I stop by and see you sometimes? Maybe take you out on a date?"

Why not? Jaycee thought.

"I'd like that," she said, squeezing his hand.

JAYCEE LED Luna from the barn and into the horse trailer, tying her up securely in the stall next to Monkeyshines before stepping out to fasten the trailer door. The two horses nosed each other with a friendly nicker. Jaycee watched them for a second, then walked around to climb into the driver's seat. Megan was in the truck, waiting for her.

"We'll see you in town at the hotel!" her mother called from the door of the house. "Have a safe trip!"

Jaycee waved and turned over the ignition as Megan tuned into Country 105 on the radio. They sang along to the top forty as they headed to Calgary and the Stampede grounds. Megan rolled down her window and hand-surfed in time to the music.

As she drove, Jaycee was preoccupied with how she would manage to finish her routine when it came time to perform. She hadn't been able to overcome her fear of doing the Death Drag, and she wondered if she should cut it completely from her repertoire. It was a popular trick, a definite crowd pleaser. Regular rodeo fans would expect to see it done during a trick riding routine. Could she compensate with some other combination of tricks? Probably not. Would the Stampede committee invite her again if she didn't perform as expected? Doubtful. She would have to get a handle on this.

"What's with the sad face, girl?" Megan asked. "Aren't you looking forward to hitting Ranchman's tonight? Afraid you'll be a wallflower?"

Jaycee looked over and replaced her frown with a grin. "What if I am? No cowboy is safe around you, Megan Burns! I'll be entertained just watching you work the room!"

Megan laughed loudly. "You said it, cowgirl! It's a matter of separating out the best bulls from the herd and then puttin' your brand on their butt."

"Well, you watch yourself. You know most of them are looking for an easy lay during Stampede, and there's you crying in your beer at the end of the week. Remember last year?"

Megan waved her hand dismissively. "Oh, that! I was over him in two days."

"Two days of swearing off men, as I remember? Then you found another one."

Megan smiled, remembering. "Jack Henderson. He was pretty cute, all right. I wonder if he'll be back this year?"

Jaycee shook her finger at her friend. "You broke his heart. I saw his face when you said goodbye."

"Yeah, there was something about him," said Megan, thoughtfully. "I don't know. He was different. Nice. Maybe too nice. I like the bad boys!"

"Yep, I noticed." Jaycee cocked an eyebrow and smirked. "You're not getting any younger, you know! Don't you want to settle down and have kids?" This was Jaycee's secret dream, but it was somehow too sacred to share even with Megan.

"Oh, plenty of time for that," Megan replied. "I want to sow some wild oats before I plant my home field."

"You'll have plenty of opportunities at Ranchman's," Jaycee observed.

"Yeeeehaaaaw! I can't wait!" Megan shrilled. "It's about time you had some fun, too, Jaycee. You've haven't really kicked up your heels since..." Megan stopped suddenly and was swept by a wave of guilt when she saw Jaycee's expression. Her voice dropped a tone. "I'm so, so sorry, Jaycee, I just..."

"Never mind, Megan, it's okay. I need to get my feet under me again, is all. I want to enjoy Stampede this year if I can."

They travelled the last miles into Calgary in silence. Finally, they pulled into the Stampede grounds, showing their identification to the gate attendant.

At the barns, they found their stall numbers and unloaded the horses, making sure there was enough feed and water before going to the hotel to meet Jaycee's parents at the Marriott Hotel.

ELLIS MCRAE WAS SITTING in the hotel lounge nursing a glass of Laphroaig, savoring each sip of the fine Scotch whisky as he waited for his wife. He took advantage of this quiet moment to think about Jaycee. He knew she was struggling emotionally.

Ever since last year, he'd been preoccupied with his grief, and that of his wife. He'd let Jaycee down. She had lost confidence and he was at a loss to know how to help her. He had seen the terror on her face when she had come to the part of her routine where she usually performed the Death Drag. After last year, how could she help but feel that way?

She had been riding since she was a little bit of a girl, and had always been at home in the saddle. Then everything had changed in their world. He had to admit he felt fear when watching her practice, but he vowed he would never let her see it in him.

Ruth slid down on to the chair next to his.

"Laphroaig?" she asked. He nodded. After a year of hard work on the ranch, staying in town at a good hotel, enjoying fine meals and treating themselves had always been their tradition during Stampede week.

"Want one?" he asked. She nodded. Ellis waved the waitress over and ordered a second whisky for his wife.

"I've been thinking about Jaycee," he said.

Ruth nodded. "I know she's having a hard time."

"She is. She still can't do the Death Drag in her practice."

Ruth shook her head. "How will she be able to do her routine in the arena if she can't do it at home? She's always been so fearless, Ellis. I'm worried." Ruth turned her head away and took out a tissue to wipe a tear away.

Ellis reached for her hand. "I know, love. I know."

Ruth clasped his hand tight and only released it when the waitress brought her drink.

"To our girls," she said, lifting the glass.

"Our girls," Ellis responded.

JAYCEE AND MEGAN joined them in the restaurant an hour later.

"How was the drive?" Ruth asked.

"It was fine. The horses are settled in," Jaycee replied.

"I'm starved!" said Megan. "What's good?"

"Try the steak. They prepare it nice and rare here," Ellis suggested.

"Sounds great, Mr. McRae. Jaycee, what'll you have?"

Jaycee reviewed the menu for a few seconds.

"I'll go for the pasta carbonara," she finally decided. "...and a glass of Chardonnay."

Ellis caught the attention of the waiter. "So, what are you girls up to tonight?"

"Ranchman's, of course!" Megan grinned.

Ruth and Ellis exchanged smiles. They remembered many a fine night out country dancing. Back in the day they had even done some exhibition dancing: two-step, waltz, swing, schottische.

"I remember the first time I saw your Mama in there," Ellis said. "The men were falling all over themselves to get to her."

Ruth slapped his arm. "Oh, come on! You know I only had eyes for one cowboy. The best calf roper in Southern Alberta, I think he was."

"We sure cut a rug in them days," Ellis remembered.

"And that's what we plan to do tonight!" Megan said, chuckling.

"Wooee, watch out, pardners! Hang on to your belt buckles!" Ellis teased her. He noticed Jaycee was quiet, looking down at her hands.

"Yep, this buckle bunny is on the hop tonight!" Megan glanced over at Jaycee. "Right, Jaycee?"

"Right," Jaycee responded, looking up with a forced smile. "Like I said, it's the best show in town watching you work the floor at Ranchman's."

"Well, you girls be careful," Ruth interjected. "Keep your wits about you."

"Always." Jaycee winked at her mother, with a false gaiety that didn't fool anyone.

IT WASN'T easy finding parking during Stampede, but Jaycee and Megan finally made it to the club. They heard the pounding music and roar of conversation even before they opened the door. It was packed, a sea of Stetson hats, colorful shirts, jeans, short skirts, glittery tops, cutoffs and cowboy boots. The dance floor was a revolving swirl of movement, with dance partners executing complex turns and moves despite the tightness of the space.

"Let's find a table!" Megan shouted in Jaycee's ear. They wound their way through the crowd to the bar, ordered a couple of beers, and soon were ensconced at a table next to the dance floor. Within minutes, Megan was asked to dance and Jaycee watched her disappear into the crowd.

"Dance?" Jaycee looked up to see a familiar face.

"Jack?" she asked. "Jack Henderson?"

"At your service." Jack performed a gracious bow. "Care to join me?"

Jaycee took his outreached hand. Within seconds they were two-stepping their way around the dance floor.

"So, how have you been, Jack?" Jaycee shouted.

"Just dandy, ma'am. And you?"

"I'm doin' great, thanks."

"I was sorry to hear about—"

"Yes, thanks, Jack." Her tone told him that this was a topic to stay away from.

"Performing this year?" he asked.

"Um, I think so," Jaycee murmured.

"Pardon?" Jack yelled.

"I THINK SO."

Jack smiled and twirled her around a few times before speaking again.

"Is your buddy with you?" he asked. Jaycee had known this was coming.

"She's around here somewhere," Jaycee replied.

At the end of the dance, Jack escorted her back to her table. Megan was already there.

"Why, Jack Henderson, I swear!" Megan said, looking up at Jack coquettishly. They locked eyes.

"Megan, good to see you," Jack replied. There was an awkward silence as they stared at each other. Jaycee could feel the tension between them. Jack was the first to break it.

"Well, gotta go. I told my buddy I'd buy him a beer," Jack explained. "Dance later, Megan?"

"I'd like that," Megan replied.

"Okay, later," Jack said, then quickly turned on his heel and disappeared into the throng.

"Careful, Megan," Jaycee said. "Don't you break that man's heart again."

Jaycee was surprised that instead of the usual quick comeback, Megan was serious.

"Yeah, you're right. I'll be careful."

"Good girl."

By ten o'clock, Jaycee could see Megan looking around for Jack and the promised dance. Megan was ripping the label off her beer bottle, bit by bit.

"He'll get here," Jaycee finally said. "Don't worry."

"Who?" Megan was feigning disinterest.

"Jack."

"Oh that. I was looking around to see if I knew anybody at the bar."

"Uh huh." As soon as she said this, Jaycee saw Jack making a beeline for their table. Megan sat up and pretended to be looking somewhere else.

"Ready for that dance, Megan?" Jack was at the table, holding out his hand.

"Oh yeah, I forgot. Don't mind if I do, Jack," Megan said nonchalantly. Taking his hand, she stood up and followed him onto the dance floor.

She really likes that guy, Jaycee thought. *It would be nice to see her find a good man and settle down a bit.* Megan's impulsiveness and crazy antics had gotten her in trouble ever since Jaycee could remember. Megan had been popular in high school, but at a price. Her reputation had suffered and she still struggled with self-esteem. Jaycee knew she was lonely, although Megan would never have admitted it. Jaycee had been her rock, the one friend Megan ran to when things went sideways, as they often did. She saw Jack and Megan come past as they circled the floor. Jack was smiling ear to ear, his focus on his partner, with Megan looking everywhere but at him. *Oh damn*, Jaycee thought, *here we go again, just like last year. Don't lead the guy on, Megan!*

She glanced around the room. In the corner, she noticed a handsome dark-haired man sitting with a group of other men. He was staring directly at her. Unlike his friends, who were waving their arms around and engaging in what appeared to be a lively debate, the dark man sat quietly. He had a presence and an intensity that Jaycee could not ignore. Suddenly, he rose and headed straight for her table. *Oh my God*, Jaycee thought. She hadn't intended to engage his attention, but maybe she had held his gaze a bit too long?

His dark good looks took her breath away. She could see a strong, athletic body, with wide shoulders, a slim waist, and tight thighs. His clothes seemed a little different from what she was used to. The next thing she knew he was in front of her, holding out his hand.

"Dance?" he said, his eyebrows elevated and a slight smile on his lips. He had an accent of some sort. She couldn't quite place it but knew she had heard this kind of accent before. She put her hand in his and was on the dance floor and in his muscular arms within seconds. It was a two-step. He was a superb lead.

She smiled up at him. "You dance well."

"Thank you," he answered. "We learned when we were young, all the dances, at our school."

What was that accent?

"Oh yes? Where did you go to school?" she asked.

"Russia."

So he was Russian. That was it. Eastern European.

"I don't meet too many people from Russia. Are you here for the Stampede?"

"*Da*," he replied. "And you?"

"Yes… at least I think so." Jaycee immediately felt stupid as she saw the confusion on his face. "That is, I'm supposed to be performing, but I… I'm not sure if I can. I'm a trick rider."

She could see interest in his expression. "You're injured?"

She shook her head, then surprised herself with her answer.

"No," she said, uncomfortable, glancing away, "it's just that… well, I'm afraid."

Why was she telling him this? Because it's easier to tell a stranger? She had no clue, she somehow knew in her heart she could confide in him.

He looked at her thoughtfully. "*Da*, I understand. I too am a trick rider."

Jaycee was surprised to hear this. The song ended and was followed by a waltz. He kept her on the dance floor. She was glad. As he drew her close, she felt the hardness of his body against hers. A sudden thrill ran through her. She felt a surge of sexual longing, an old familiar ache. She closed her eyes. It was lust, and it felt great, because it took her mind away from her troubles. Suddenly she wanted sex, just pure sex. No strings. It had been a long time… in fact, she couldn't quite remember when the last time was.

When the waltz ended, she felt regret as he walked her off the dance floor. Her body was still thrumming with desire.

"Wait, what's your name?" Jaycee asked before he could walk away. It seemed kind of silly under the circumstances, but she must find out.

"Sergei. Sergei Volkov." He looked down at her. "And you?"

"Jaycee McRae."

"Well, Miss Jaycee McRae, perhaps we will see each other again?"

Jaycee looked at him intently. "I hope so."

"Me also."

She watched him walk back to his table and immediately heard the shouts and teasing of his companions as he took his seat. They toasted him, grinning, and looked over their shoulders toward her. She felt embarrassed and was grateful when Megan suddenly reappeared and sat down beside her.

~

"HOW WAS YOUR DANCE?" Jaycee turned to her friend.

"More importantly, how was yours?" Megan shot back with a grin. "And who is that gorgeous man I saw you dancing with?"

Jaycee found herself blushing. "His name is Sergei. He's from Russia."

Megan clapped her hands together. "Russian! How exotic!" She looked over at the table where Sergei and his friends were sitting. "Wow, a whole table of handsome Russians. Look at 'em!"

"Megan…" Jaycee said, a tone of warning in her voice.

"Oh, come on, Jaycee, share the bounty!" Megan laughed.

"What about Jack?" Jaycee asked.

Megan faltered. "Jack? Oh, I don't know."

This was unlike Megan. She was usually very definite when it came to men she was interested in.

"Do you have feelings for him, Megan?" Jaycee leaned closer to catch Megan's answer above the noise.

Megan rolled her eyes. "Oh, hell, I don't know. There's something about that guy. He unsettles me, Jaycee."

"So it seems," Jaycee observed, grinning.

"I know what you're thinking. And believe me, I'll keep my distance so I don't hurt his feelings."

"That's up to you, Megan. I think he's a pretty good guy, but only you can decide whose boots fit best under your bed."

"I need to think on it, okay?"

"Of course, but be careful."

"I will."

Jaycee and Megan were kept busy dancing with various partners for the next couple of hours. At some point, Jaycee looked over and saw that the table full of Russian men had left. She felt a pang of disappointment. Would she ever see Sergei again? At the end of the night, Jack reappeared to dance with Megan one last time. Jaycee knew he was playing it cool. Smart guy. That was the best way to keep Megan's attention. When the dance was finished, Jaycee saw Megan and Jack talking for a couple of minutes on the dance floor before Megan came back to the table and picked up her jean jacket off the chair back.

"Ready to hit the road?" she asked.

"Ready." Jaycee put on her own jacket and slung her purse over her shoulder.

She deliberately didn't ask about Megan's conversation with Jack, though she could tell that Megan was brooding over it.

Whatever it was, Megan didn't share it with Jaycee on the drive back to the hotel. After parking the car, the two women hugged each other, said goodnight and went off to their respective hotel rooms.

CHAPTER 4

*J*aycee was up bright and early the next morning. She was helping herself to coffee and the complimentary continental breakfast when Megan joined her in the hotel café.

"What are your plans today?" Megan asked, pouring a waterfall of sugar into her coffee. Jaycee could never understand how Megan could drink her coffee with that much sweetness in it. Like drinking syrup. But Megan seemed to thrive on it.

"Over to the barns, check on Luna, then I'll probably spend the day practicing. You?"

"Same. I want Monkey to get familiar with the arena and the barrels before he has to be in front of the crowd. Where's your mom and dad?" Megan asked.

"Sleeping in, or what they call sleeping in," Jaycee replied. "Neither can sleep past six normally, but my guess is they are treating themselves to room service."

"Maybe they just want to get frisky!" Megan joked.

Jaycee rolled her eyes. "Oh man. Let's not go there, okay? Too much information!"

Megan laughed. "Okay." She took a long sip of her sugary coffee and bit into a croissant. "Want to drive over together?"

"Sure," Jaycee agreed.

AT THE BARNS, Luna put her head over the stall door as she saw Jaycee come in.

"Hello, sweet girl." Jaycee rubbed Luna's nose and offered her some pieces of apple she had grabbed out of the fruit basket at the café.

Luna munched up the treat eagerly. Jaycee slipped a halter over her head and led her out to be saddled.

Megan was doing exactly the same with Monkeyshines.

After outfitting Luna, Jaycee ran her hand lovingly across the beautiful white leather trick saddle she had inherited from her mother. It had been repaired and modified over the years until it was customized for her specific use, and she loved it. A good horse, a good saddle, confidence and skill. These, her mother had taught her, were the best safety nets for a trick rider. But now her confidence was gone, putting her at risk. She simply had to get it back.

In a dark corner of the stall, she pulled her training clothes out of a duffel bag, changed quickly and led Luna out to the training paddock. Soon she had Luna galloping a steady circuit and began to work through her routine. After three tries, Jaycee still couldn't bring herself to do the Death Drag. It was like she was frozen to the saddle every time she came close to it.

She was so absorbed in the problem that at first she didn't see the man standing near the fence. When she did notice him, her heart jumped in her chest. It was Sergei Volkov.

JAYCEE SLOWED Luna down and cantered over to where Sergei was standing.

"We meet again." Sergei smiled up at her. "You're a good rider."

"Thank you." Jaycee smiled back.

"And we do some of the same tricks," Sergei observed.

Jaycee dismounted, patted Luna's neck and stood facing him across the fence.

"How was I?" she asked.

Sergei hesitated, then spoke. "You ride well, but I see you hold back sometimes."

Was it that obvious?

"I'm warming up, that's all," Jaycee said defensively.

"Of course. *Da.*" Sergei stroked Luna's nose. "You have a good horse."

"Her name's Luna."

Sergei gently bent one of Luna's ears toward him. "Good Luna. Good girl." Then he whispered softly in Russian.

As if to answer, Luna immediately touched Sergei's shoulder with her nose and nibbled his hair. Jaycee had never seen her horse respond so quickly to another person. Usually Luna was a bit skittish around strangers. Not so with this man.

"You have a special way with horses," Jaycee said.

"They are like my brothers and sisters," Sergei replied. "Since I was a small boy, I'd sleep in stable, not in the house." He grinned.

"As long as you ate and bathed in the house," said Jaycee, smiling. "I have no problem with that!"

Sergei laughed heartily. "*Da*, I'd eat in the house, and take baths, at least sometimes." He cast her a teasing look. "So you can come near me, don't be afraid."

If he only knew how much she wanted to 'come near' him! She remembered her lusty thoughts when they had danced together. She watched as Sergei ran his strong hand along Luna's neck. *What would it be like to have that hand stroking her?*

"I'll go now." Sergei reached across the fence and pushed a

strand of hair away from Jaycee's face. It was an intimate gesture which made her pulse race, and the warmth in his eyes was unmistakable. "Keep practicing. We Volkovs practice this afternoon, at another paddock near here. Will you come and watch us?"

"I will, if you want me to."

Sergei nodded and gave her directions. "We will talk again, afterwards."

"Yes." She didn't know why or how, but this man was completely spellbinding. She could no more deny him than fly to the moon.

LATER THAT AFTERNOON, Jaycee watched the Volkov troupe practice. She was astonished at their technical expertise. The troupe did tricks in pairs and even in threes. Seeing three men standing in a perfect pyramid on two horses in the Hippodrome Stand was new to her. In the past, she and her sister had done some tandem trick riding, but nothing at this level. She couldn't take her eyes off the Russians, watching every move carefully with a view to improving her own technique or adding something interesting to her routine.

Across the paddock, she saw a young woman, close to her own age, holding some of the troupe's horses. Even at a distance Jaycee could see that she was beautiful, with a long slim body and a cascade of blonde hair that flowed past her waist.

For some reason, the woman was looking back at Jaycee with an angry expression. *What's her problem?* Jaycee wondered. *I'm only watching.*

Then a thought occurred to her. *Maybe she's Sergei's girlfriend or wife?* Jaycee realized she knew very little about Sergei. He could be attached or married. Some performers didn't wear rings or other jewelry as a safety measure. But the way he had looked at her, both at Ranchman's and this morning at the paddock, made her think he was attracted to her. Was she imagining things?

Suddenly, there was Sergei was looking down at her from the saddle, a big grin on his face.

"You're here."

"Your troupe is phenomenal!" Jaycee said enthusiastically.

"Thank you. They work hard."

"You do some tricks I've never seen." Jaycee reached over to pet his horse's velvety nose.

"I can teach you, if you wish."

Seeing the woman still glaring at her, Jaycee hastily changed the subject. "What's your horse's name?"

"Pasha. He's a good horse. I trained him myself."

"He has a smooth gait and seems to anticipate you. You make a great team," Jaycee observed.

Sergei agreed. "*Da*, that's why I picked him. We know each other well, and he has a sweet temper."

Sergei's father and brothers rode over to join Sergei and were introduced to Jaycee.

"We like your country very much," Mikhail said with enthusiasm.

"I'm glad," Jaycee answered. She turned toward Sergei's father. "Mr. Volkov, your troupe is wonderful. I can learn so much watching you."

Petr smiled at her. "*Spasebo*, Miss McRae. We are happy to be here."

Across the paddock, Jaycee saw the blonde woman wave her hand and heard her call Sergei's name.

"I must go," Sergei said, glancing over. "You wait. I'll come back soon to talk. Okay?"

"Yes."

The four men turned their horses and rode toward the barn.

∾

ABOUT TWENT MINUTES LATER, Sergei returned. At his suggestion, he and Jaycee walked to one of the nearby concessions to get coffee. Carrying their paper cups to a picnic table, they discussed the various tricks and routines familiar to both of them. Jaycee asked him a few technical questions.

"You're avoiding something in your routine, *da*? The thing that gives you fear?" Sergei asked, looking at her intently. "I see you start, then you hold back."

Jaycee closed her eyes for a moment. When she opened them again, she saw he was leaning toward her with a sympathetic look in his eyes. Should she tell him? Maybe talking would help.

"It's the Death Drag, or Suicide Drag, as some people call it." Jaycee had seen him perform it perfectly in his routine during the Volkovs' practice session.

Sergei nodded. "This is a dangerous trick."

Jaycee hesitated, wondering how much she should share. This was difficult, but she needed him to understand why she was so afraid.

"Someone I loved…" she started and was mortified when her voice broke. She couldn't go on.

Sergei immediately reached across the table, laying his hand over hers. "It's okay, Jaycee. I understand. An accident?" Jaycee nodded, still unable to speak. The two sat silently for a few minutes.

"My sister, Kerrie," Jaycee finally said, a single tear running down her cheek. "She was only twenty-five."

He waited for her to continue.

"She caught her foot in the saddle. It took time to stop the horse. We got her to the hospital but…" Her face crumpled.

Finally, he spoke, quietly and gently. "Jaycee, I will tell you about my mama. She was a good rider. Always careful. But, one day, her horse fell. An accident. That was the end."

"I'm sorry, Sergei," Jaycee said. "How old were you?"

"Fourteen. My brothers were twelve and nine years old."

"How awful for all of you."

"Papa did not do well. He got sick. We boys had to help him and hold the family together. We kept riding, kept performing. It was difficult." He looked deeply into her eyes. "Jaycee, this is what we must come to accept in this work. It is not always safe. Mama wanted her boys to be good men, and good riders. She trained us well, and she knew the danger."

"I understand."

"And you, Jaycee? Do you have other brothers or sisters?"

"I only had Kerrie. Her death was painful for all of us, especially my parents."

"And for you, still."

"Yes."

"And the fear comes from this? When you are riding?"

Jaycee looked into his eyes. He really did understand.

"Yes. It's only been a year since it happened. We miss her so much, and yes, I am terrified of doing the Death Drag in my routine."

They sat quietly for a few minutes. Jaycee decided to move on to another subject. "Sergei, who is the woman I saw at practice today?"

Sergei hesitated, but only for a split second. Still, Jaycee noticed it. "Her name is Irina Petrov. She and Vladimir Ivanovich are also performers in our troupe. So, will you let me help?"

Jaycee was confused. "Help with what?"

"The trick. I can help. We'll practice. I'll coach you."

Jaycee looked up at him. This was unexpected. "Are you sure you have the time? You must be preparing for the rodeo yourself."

"I have time. We can meet tomorrow morning, okay? At your paddock."

Jaycee wasn't at all sure about his offer, but it was worth a try. She decided to take the risk.

"Okay," she answered.

"See you at eight o'clock." He patted her hand, smiling broadly.

CHAPTER 5

*P*etr Volkov opened the door to his hotel room and Vladimir Ivanovich stepped in. In the darkness outside the window, the lights of the city glimmered.

"Vodka?" Petr asked.

Vladimir nodded.

Petr walked over to the desk where a large bottle of vodka sat with two glasses. He poured a generous measure into each glass while Vladimir seated himself at the table near the window, then brought the drinks to the table and sat down.

Both men raised their glasses.

"*Za zdorov'ye!*" They downed the vodka and slammed the glasses down.

Vladimir leaned forward. "We need to make a plan, Petr. My friends will be here soon and you will have to deal with your problem as I have advised."

Petr shook his head. "Is there no other way?"

"You must do as I suggest."

"I can't. What will happen to my sons?"

"It's too late for that. If you don't take care of this, you'll lose everything. You may even go to prison, or worse. My friends can help."

"Your friends are criminals."

"True. But they can fix this."

"The price is too high."

"There is no other way, and I am the only one who can arrange it."

Petr leaned forward and rubbed his hands over his face. He cursed under his breath. "What will I tell Sergei?"

"Never mind Sergei." Vladimir got up and fetched the bottle from the desk, pouring them a second drink. "You will know what to say when the time comes. Now drink, and we will make a plan."

THE NEXT MORNING, Jaycee was up early and at the paddock, warming up Luna and waiting for Sergei. She was thinking of their conversation the previous day. She had surprised herself by the ease with which she could open up and share her life with a man she hardly knew. Yet somehow it had seemed natural. After all, Sergei was a trick rider, like herself. If anyone could identify with her fears and lack of confidence, it was him. He had suffered loss, as she had. Remembering the compassion in his eyes and the touch of his hand on hers, Jaycee admitted to herself that she had a strong attraction to him. She was nervous about seeing him again.

Finally, she saw Sergei walking toward the paddock. Filled with hope and excitement, she reined Luna over to the fence to meet him.

Sergei smiled up at her. "Now, we begin, *da?*"

"Yes, I'm ready." Jaycee smiled back and gave him her full attention.

"Today, we will practice back bends. Five back bends, then you come to the fence and we'll talk."

Jaycee nodded, relieved. This she could handle. At his signal, she took Luna into a gallop and performed the back bends as instructed.

"How did that feel?" Sergei asked.

"It felt okay," Jaycee replied.

"Now, again, but this time bend back farther each time. As far as you can bend."

Once again, Jaycee performed as Sergei had instructed her. Leaning farther and farther back, she began to feel the familiar panic, but suffered through it until she had completed her task.

"And now?" Sergei asked.

"I felt a bit of panic," Jaycee admitted.

"Okay. We'll do this once again, Jaycee, bending back as far as you can," Sergei instructed.

This time Jaycee bent back as far as she possibly could. The panic was definitely there, but it had lessened a bit.

"That was better," she reported.

"That's enough for today," Sergei said.

Jaycee was surprised. "That's it?"

"*Da*. We'll practice again tomorrow, but I want you to do something. This afternoon, lie on your bed, on your back. Close your eyes and imagine. Feel the horse, feel the motion and speed, hear the sound of hooves. When you are ready, imagine yourself performing the Death Drag. Take time to feel everything, good or bad. Then open your eyes. Know you are safe. Do this many times. Then rest."

Jaycee looked doubtful. "I guess I can try it," she said.

"No trying, you must do this for me." He was serious.

She nodded. Even the prospect of visualizing the Death Drag made her feel a cold dread inside. Still, she was ready to do anything to get her nerve back.

"I'll do it, Sergei. I promise."

Sergei nodded. He looked at her with pride in his eyes. "You've done well today. I'll take you out tonight for a meal, and we can talk more. Now, go home and practice." He reached up and squeezed her hand.

Jaycee felt a flood of emotion. *He really wants to help me with this. And he wants to take me to dinner! Does that mean he feels attracted, too?*

"Thank you, Sergei. I'm very grateful."

Sergei's expression softened even more. "Okay. We'll meet here tonight at seven o'clock."

"Okay." She was excited at the prospect of seeing him again. "Tonight."

BACK AT THE HOTEL, Jaycee closed the curtains and lay on her back on the bed. Taking a few deep breaths, she closed her eyes and began to imagine the familiar movement and heat of Luna's body as they galloped around the paddock. It didn't take long for the visualization to take effect. She felt her body bounce against Luna's side, heard the familiar hoofbeats and felt the wind in her hair. Then she visualized hooking her right foot and leg under the saddle strap as she arched backward. Her leg tensed, taking the full weight of her body as she pointed her left leg straight upwards. She arched her back and released her hands downward.

Suddenly, Jaycee felt a stabbing pain in her chest and could not get her breath. She jerked up in the bed, gasping for air, her heart racing.

She closed her eyes. *Damn.* Then the memories began to come, and she couldn't push them down.

Stampede. Last year.

Jaycee stood by the fence at the bottom of the grandstand, watching with pride as her sister, Kerrie, performed her last routine of the day. Trick after trick, the crowd roared its approval.

The finale was coming. Giving a jaunty wave, Kerrie hooked her right foot under the saddle strap and dropped backward into the Death Drag, hanging upside down with her arms over her head, her left leg pointed up and her hands almost dragging in the dirt. It was a spectacular trick that both she and Kerrie liked to use at the end of their routines. Both women had done it hundreds of times.

Wait. Something wasn't right.

Her sister was in trouble. Jaycee watched with mounting terror as Kerrie sat part way up and desperately tried to free her right leg, which was caught at an awkward angle. Suddenly Kerrie's body dropped as the leg released and Kerrie lost her grip on the saddle. Her right foot remained caught. Unable to right herself, Kerrie's body was dragging beside the horse, her head and upper body bouncing and slamming down into the dirt. She looked like a rag doll, arms flailing as her horse galloped faster.

At first Jaycee was completely frozen, watching the horrific event unfold as if in slow motion. The next thing she knew she was in the arena, running toward Kerrie's horse with her arms out in a futile effort to stop it. The horse shied away as it galloped past her. Jaycee caught a glimpse of Kerrie's unconscious face. The shouts and screams of the crowd sounded far away, as if she was hearing them underwater.

Several men ran into the arena. The announcer was trying to calm the crowd. Two cowboys quickly roped Kerrie's horse and brought it to a halt. One of the cowboys threw a cloth over the horse's eyes as more men ran to help and the stretcher crew arrived. Jaycee put her hands over her face. She couldn't bear to watch. She could hear someone screaming. Later she realized the screams were her own.

Finally the men got Kerrie onto the stretcher. As the stretcher crew raced for the exit, Jaycee ran alongside, looking down at her sister's face and hair covered in dirt and matted with blood. So much blood, and Kerrie's lips were blue. Was this really happening?

Jaycee begged to come in the ambulance. The EMTs didn't want to spend time arguing with her. They exchanged grim glances and agreed, telling her to keep out of the way. She squashed herself in a corner, watching the EMTs try to resuscitate Kerrie's limp body. The siren blared, the rig shook, and the EMTs shouted orders to each other. She couldn't even touch Kerrie, who was blocked from her view. Where were her parents?

Ellis and Ruth arrived at the hospital shortly after the ambulance, their faces gray and drawn with anxiety. They had not been in the arena at the time of the accident and had been notified by the police. A doctor came out to tell them Kerrie was still in surgery. His serious manner alarmed them even more. Would Kerrie be all right? It was too early to say. Jaycee went to the cafeteria to get coffee and the long vigil began. No one wanted to eat. After an excruciatingly long night in the waiting room, the arrival of a new shift of medical staff told them that morning had come.

Finally a doctor, dressed in green scrubs and a surgical cap, walked slowly down the hall towards them. His head was down, and Jaycee was unable to read his face. As soon as he looked up, she knew the outcome, and so did her parents.

"I'm so sorry," the doctor said, quietly. "We did everything within our power to save her, but her injuries were too severe." Jaycee watched as her mother collapsed against her father. Kerrie, her dear little sister, was dead.

Dead.

Now, a year later, Jaycee sat in her hotel room, remembering all of it. The numbness and disbelief. The silence and the empty chair at the dinner table. Phoning the relatives. Arranging the funeral. Watching the coffin being lowered into the ground. The weeks when she was too afraid to ride. The long slow process of starting to practice again, this time as a solo act.

Jaycee jumped up from the bed and ran into the bathroom. She vomited and leaned against the cold porcelain of the toilet, trying to recover her breath. Then she cried, the long mournful cries of a wounded animal.

~

SEVEN O'CLOCK CAME and went as Sergei waited at the paddock. By eight o'clock, he realized that Jaycee was not coming. And he didn't know where to find her.

Sergei was furious with himself. Why hadn't he asked for her phone number? For the name of her hotel? He slammed his hand against the fence and turned to walk back to his RV. Maybe she got delayed? Or worse, was in an accident?

Or maybe she simply didn't want to come? He only wanted to help her.

No. That was wrong. He wanted more. He wanted to take her into his arms and hold her close, stroke her hair and reassure her that everything would be all right. And then make long, slow passionate love to her. Though he had enjoyed many lovers in the past, he had never met a woman who fascinated him as Jaycee did. He could not stop thinking about her. There was something so honest, so real about her. Now he felt he had underestimated how fragile she was emotionally. Her loss was so recent. Maybe she wasn't ready to push herself into performing a trick that terrified her. Was he putting her in danger by making her try?

CHAPTER 6

The next morning, Irina Petrov twirled her long blonde hair up onto the top of her head and fastened it with a hair elastic. She put on her work gloves and picked up a pitchfork, ready to muck out the Volkov horse stalls. Down the length of the barn she could see Sergei and his brother, Mikhail, working the stalls at the other end. It was a hot day, and both men had their shirts off. Irina was in a skimpy and revealing white tank top, which she hoped Sergei would notice. She took a few moments to watch him. His tanned, rippling arm and back muscles flexed as he wielded his fork. Sergei looked up suddenly. Irina just as quickly turned and stuck her fork in the dirty straw of the first stall.

Yes, she had big plans for Sergei, and it certainly didn't hurt that he was so good-looking. She could almost, but not quite, give up her current lover, Vladimir, for such a prize. Still, it would be fun to seduce Sergei, as Vlad had asked her to do. Whatever happened, Irina would keep Vlad informed. Vladimir Ivanovich already owned her heart and her body, but none of the Volkovs knew it. She and Vlad had been careful to hide their relationship so they could work more effectively on their common goal, taking control of the Volkov troupe.

Vlad was already blackmailing Petr. In the meantime, she planned to enjoy herself with Sergei. She was confident in using her abundant sexual prowess to manipulate and distract him from his responsibilities in running the troupe. She knew exactly how to make a man crazy with desire. Then, after she had bedded Sergei, she would share her sexual adventures with Vladimir. It would be a real turn on.

At the moment, she had to figure out how to get Sergei to spend more time with her. She had made some overtures on the plane from Russia but didn't get the response she hoped for. And now that Canadian woman was in the picture. She could see that Sergei liked the woman and had even begun to coach her. That was bad. Irina needed to find a way to stop it, before Sergei got too involved. The Canadian was certainly attractive, but Irina was practiced in the art of drawing a man's attention away from everything else.

She looked down the barn and smiled at Sergei when he looked up. He grinned back.

"I'll beat you to the middle!" Irina yelled. Sergei and Mikhail couldn't resist. They nodded and all three started forking the straw even faster. She knew that she couldn't keep up with them, but that was part of her plan. It would work either way. If she did win, she could offer to buy drinks. If not, she knew these men loved to be gracious to a loser, especially if it was a woman.

All of them were sweating freely now. Soon Irina's clingy top began to show every detail of the flesh underneath. She wasn't wearing a bra, a deliberate choice on her part. By the time the men reached the middle stall and threw their arms into the air in triumph, she was still two stalls away, and soaked to the skin.

Irina laughed. "Okay, you win! But you have to make up for it, or my heart will be broken." She gave Sergei an inviting look combined with a sexy pout on her beautifully plump lips.

Sergei had indeed noticed. In fact, she could see that both brothers' eyes were on her hardened nipples, clearly outlined under her sweat-soaked top. *Men were so predictable.* She ran her hands down her body provocatively until her fingers rested on her hips.

"I'll take you out for a cold beer, Irina!" Mikhail said eagerly.

"We'll all go," Irina suggested. Both men nodded as they wiped their foreheads with the back of their hands. "There's a good place not far from here."

IRINA, Sergei and Dmitri sat in the dark bar, enjoying ice cold Canadian beer, which was a novelty to all of them. It was the perfect drink after a long morning of physical work.

Mikhail couldn't take his eyes off Irina. *I'll have to watch him,* Sergei thought, *or he'll get into trouble.*

"Don't you love this place?" Irina was enthusiastic. Sergei knew she was talking about the country, not the bar. "People here do what they want, go where they want, say what they want! Such freedom! What do you think, Sergei?"

Sergei agreed. "It's a good country. The people are very friendly."

This made Irina frown. "What do you mean? Who?"

Sergei took another sip of his beer. "Everyone I've met so far. Friendly."

Irina decided to let it drop and turned to Mikhail. "What do you think, *Misha*?"

Mikhail was enthusiastic. "Yes, there's so much opportunity! I could live in a place like this, but Papa would never consider it." He flagged down the waiter to order another round.

"How do you know? Maybe you should talk to him about it." Irina put her hand over Mikhail's and the young man grinned, pleased at the attention. He glanced over at Sergei, who looked back at him and shook his head. "We have a job to do here, Mikhail. We are here to represent our country. That's all. Irina, stop putting ideas in his head."

Irina turned away from Mikhail to face him, smiling coyly.

"Sergei, let the man dream. This is a big adventure for him. For all of us."

"I agree, but for now, we need to keep our focus on our work. We need to perform well and conduct ourselves appropriately."

Now Irina's hand was on Sergei's arm. "Oh come on, Sergei! What an old man you are! You are too serious. We can do all that and enjoy ourselves as well. Why not think big?"

"We can talk about it later."

It was Mikhail's turn to speak. "Sergei, Irina is right. We may not have this opportunity again. We should make some plans, make some contacts, and talk to Papa. What would it hurt?"

Sergei looked at his brother for a long moment.

"Mikhail, I understand. As I said, we'll talk later." He waved the waiter over and paid for the drinks. "Time to get back to work." Mikhail looked downcast.

"Later… later! Always later!" Irina complained. "Let him be, Sergei!"

Sergei felt guilty for discouraging his brother. He wondered what Mikhail and Irina would say if they knew that Sergei himself was already dreaming of living and working in Canada. For now, he wanted to keep things under control, and it was hard to manage with Irina upsetting his brother right before a big performance.

They pushed their chairs back and walked out into the bright July sunlight. It took a moment for their eyes to adjust.

"Irina, I want you to run through your routine this afternoon so I can see what needs to be corrected. Mikhail, I need you to speak to the veterinarian about checking the horses on the days we perform. I want the horses to stay healthy and strong."

"Yes, Sergei." Mikhail left them to visit the vet's office on the grounds.

Finding herself alone with Sergei, Irina decided to take advantage of the opportunity.

"Sergei, you are right. I'll focus on the work. I want to please you." She wound her arm through his. "But that doesn't mean we can't dream of great things. I love riding, and so do you. We could make something special together."

Sergei looked down at her. She really was a lovely woman. Strong-minded like his mother, but he was just as strong. He stopped walking and turned toward her.

"I know that, Irina. Believe me, I do. I want the best for the family and for the troupe. Do you understand? I have to think of them before I think of myself."

Irina reached up and touched his face.

"You are a true leader, Sergei. That's what I love about you. You're committed, and that's why I believe you could succeed here in Canada. Think about it, Sergei." She stood on tiptoe and kissed him gently on the lips. He hadn't expected that. He wrapped his arms around her and kissed her back, but as he did, Jaycee's face rose before him. An alarm bell went off deep inside.

He released Irina and saw her beaming up at him. Maybe his father was right. After all, she was Russian. She knew the work. She was strong. Beautiful. And oh so dangerously sexy. But she wasn't Jaycee.

CHAPTER 7

*J*aycee was in the barn, thinking of how to explain to Sergei why she hadn't shown up for their date last night. She didn't hear anyone approaching as she worked over Luna with the brush and curry comb, so she was a bit startled when someone spoke right beside her.

"You!"

Jaycee started and turned. It was the blonde woman she had seen holding the Volkovs' horses at their practice. She was quite good-looking, but at the moment her face was not friendly.

"Hello," Jaycee answered.

"I'm Irina Petrov."

"Hello, Irina. I've seen you at the paddock during practices."

"*Da*." The woman narrowed her eyes. "I saw you also. You've been practicing with Sergei."

"That's right, he's helping me with my routine." Jaycee wondered where this was going.

Irina's tone was threatening. "Sergei, he is mine. Mine. You understand? Stay away." There was no mistaking her meaning.

Jaycee immediately felt her temper rising. "Yours? Sergei doesn't seem like the sort of man who would belong to anyone."

Irina glared at her. "Sergei does not know the ways of American women. I don't like him working with you. You must stop."

Now Jaycee was really angry. "First of all, I'm not American, I'm Canadian. Secondly, I'm sorry, Irina, but no one tells me what I can and can't do."

Irina suddenly reached out and grabbed Jaycee's upper arm. She had a grip like steel.

"You listen to me! Stay away from him!"

Jaycee yanked her arm out of Irina's grasp. "You can leave any time now, Irina. I have nothing to say to you. I suggest if you have a problem, you take it up with Sergei."

"I will be watching you. Remember." And with a final scowl, Irina turned on her heel and walked away.

The nerve of that woman. Who did she think she was? Jaycee was furious. Then she had an unwelcome thought. Were Sergei and Irina actually together, as Irina had said? Sergei had never mentioned it, but then he hadn't given her a lot of information about himself. It could be true. Working together in the same troupe, day in and day out, would it be so surprising if Sergei or one of his brothers fell for their female colleague? Her heart sank. Jaycee finished grooming Luna and led her into the stall. Maybe she should ask Sergei, but she was too tired at the moment. It could wait.

CHAPTER 8

"*S*ergei?"

Sergei was bridling Pasha. He looked over his shoulder and saw that Jaycee was standing behind him in the barn.

"Jaycee, are you all right?"

Jaycee nodded. "I'm so sorry I didn't come last night. I wasn't feeling well."

"I understand. It's okay." Sergei walked up to her and took both her hands in his. Jaycee felt a ripple race up her spine. "We'll forget about it."

"I tried the exercise, but it was difficult. I don't know what to tell you. Maybe I'm not ready. Maybe I should cancel my performance."

Sergei regarded her thoughtfully. "You are the only one who can decide, Jaycee."

Jaycee squeezed his hands. "I know, Sergei, and you are being very patient with me."

Their eyes met, and in that moment, they knew that something had changed between them. This was no mere friendship, or coaching partnership. It was more, and they both felt it.

Jaycee's face reddened and she gently withdrew her hands. *Why did I do that?* she thought.

"What would you like to do, Jaycee?" Sergei asked gently.

Jaycee pondered his question for a moment. "Let's continue practicing."

A radiant grin broke over Sergei's face. "Good! Let's get started!"

They spent the rest of the morning working on Jaycee's routine. Sergei's presence had a way of calming her that helped her focus. He was encouraging, never critical. Every so often he would stop her and give some directions. By the end of the practice, she was feeling much better about everything.

"Will you be my guest in my RV for coffee?" he asked in a hopeful tone.

"I'd like that. We can talk about the practice," Jaycee said. *What I really want to do is spend more time with you, you beautiful, patient, incredibly caring man.*

As they walked to the RV, Sergei reached down and took her hand in his. She thrilled to the touch, enjoying the secure feeling of his hand covering hers. *He feels the same. He feels the same as I do!* She could hardly contain her excitement. Her heart pounded. *Could he feel her hand trembling?* They reached the RV and Sergei unlocked the door, holding it open for her. Everything inside was neat, organized and comfortable.

Sergei let go of her hand and took some coffee out of the cupboard.

Jaycee took an orange from the fruit bowl on the table and peeled it "This tastes wonderful after being in the paddock," she said, popping a piece in her mouth. "So juicy."

She broke off a section of orange and walked over to Sergei.

"Open," she said, with one eyebrow raised.

Sergei opened his mouth and she placed the dripping orange section on his tongue. Their eyes met. Jaycee's sensual gesture was an invitation, and they both knew it.

"Now you," Sergei said. He broke off another slice of the moist orange in her hand and fed it to her. Jaycee chewed it slowly, never taking her eyes from his. He drew her close. Jaycee put the orange down, wrapped her arms around his neck and kissed him, twining her tongue into his. The kiss lasted a long time. Finally, Jaycee drew away, breathless.

"You are delicious, Jaycee," Sergei said. She laughed.

"So are you, Sergei. I can't believe how lucky I am to have met you."

"Coffee?" he asked. She nodded. They sat down at the table, holding hands, completely absorbed in each other.

"Sergei, let me make up for the dinner I missed by taking you out to dinner tonight instead."

Sergei smiled. "You can show me what Canadians like to eat. I'd like that."

Jaycee was pleased that she would see him that evening, but she still had a question in her mind.

I have such strong feelings for this man. I have to ask.

"Would Irina mind us having dinner?"

Sergei looked perplexed. "Irina? Why?"

"She gave me the impression that you were seeing each other."

"She told you this?" Sergei was annoyed.

"Well, yes. She did."

Sergei shook his head and bit his lip, looking straight into her eyes. "*Nyet*, Jaycee. We are not together."

Jaycee felt relieved. *That's all I wanted to hear.*

"Okay. I know a great restaurant where the food is good and the service is excellent. It's quiet, and we can talk."

Sergei put his hand up to her cheek, leaned in and kissed her lightly. "Tonight then. I will pick you up at your hotel."

Jaycee's hands were trembling as she wrote down the address of the Marriott for him.

She knew that this evening would include much more than dinner and drinks.

CHAPTER 9

"Sergei. I need to talk to you."

Sergei was sitting on a bale of hay, cleaning tack and thinking of his upcoming dinner date with Jaycee, when his father came into the barn. The serious look on Petr's face made Sergei put down the harness he was cleaning.

"What is it, Papa?"

Still standing, Petr pushed his hair back with both hands, took a deep breath, and began.

"I have something to tell you, Sergei. It is not easy, but I need your help."

"Of course, Papa."

Petr looked down at his feet, then up again.

"I am in trouble, my son. I do not want Dmitri and Mikhail to know, for now."

"I am listening."

Sergei had not seen his father in such a state of anxiety since his mother's death.

"Sergei, I... I have been visiting the casinos in Russia. For a long time. Since Mama passed away. I could not bear the loneliness, so I began playing cards. I played with some people I should not have."

Sergei's heart sank, but he said nothing.

"I am in debt, Sergei. In debt to the casinos, and that means…"

Sergei finished the sentence. "You owe money to the mafia."

This was grave news indeed. Sergei had known others with the same problem, and most of them were now dead. Some of their family members were also dead. "Have you tried to pay it back?"

"I have, but it's the interest they demand. I can't get ahead of it."

"How much?" Sergei could barely hear Petr's next words. "What did you say, Papa?"

"Four million rubles."

Four million! How was this possible? Why had he not seen it when he'd reviewed the accounts? He sat in silence, trying to absorb this disastrous news.

"But the troupe accounts? They seem fine?"

"I have made them look that way, Sergei. I have been trying to pay the debt, but there is nothing left. They are asking for full payment now."

Sergei's pulse quickened. "Papa, they will kill you! They will kill us. You know what happens!"

Petr began to cry, something Sergei had not witnessed since his mother's funeral.

"Papa, we will think of something. We must take care of this right away."

"I'm so sorry, my son. I am a selfish old man."

"Never mind that. What is done is done. Let's talk about what we will do to fix this."

Petr hesitated before sharing the next piece of information. "Vladimir, he knows people."

"Vladimir? What people?"

"People in the organization. He is willing to help if I sign over the troupe to his friends."

This was a blow to Sergei. *Lose the family business? All that they had built over the years? So, Vladimir is a criminal. No great surprise.*

"Help how?" Sergei asked.

"He says that his friends will pay my debts if the troupe is signed over to them and…"

"And what?"

The news was getting worse and worse.

Petr looked away as he spoke. "They want to use the troupe to smuggle drugs."

"Oh my God! Papa, no! We can't do that!"

"We must."

Sergei was stunned. There was no way out, no way to win. He knew that. He had seen it back home in Russia. This was their choice: work for Vladimir's 'friends', or be killed.

"Papa, we must not tell Dmitri and Mikhail. Not yet. I'll talk to Vladimir."

"Yes, Sergei."

"Then you and I will talk."

"Yes."

Sergei suddenly realized the burden his father had been carrying, emotionally and physically. For the first time, he saw his father as an old man.

"Do not worry, Papa. Try to rest."

Petr gave him a weak smile. Sergei could see what an effort it was.

"Thank you, Sergei."

Sergei watched as his father slowly walked out of the barn.

CHAPTER 10

That evening, Jaycee took her time getting ready. She swept her glossy black hair into a chignon and fastened it with a decorative comb. She applied her makeup carefully and dotted some musky perfume behind her ears and on her pulse points. Perusing her closet, she settled on a deep crimson sleeveless dress with a plunging V-neck. She put the dress on over her favorite lacy push-up bra and matching panties, then added some thigh-high sheer black stockings and black high heels. She slid a silver cuff onto her wrist and fastened a small diamond necklace around her neck.

Sergei had only seen her in her riding clothes and with minimal makeup, so she wanted to make a good impression. She wanted to see desire reflected in his eyes. She wrapped a large cream shawl around her shoulders and flipped the end over her shoulder.

A knock came at the door of her hotel room. It was Megan.

"Whoa, where are you going?" Megan said as she walked in. "Get a load of you! Who's the lucky guy? Please tell me he's Russian!"

"As a matter of fact, he is. It's Sergei, the man I was dancing with at the bar. He's been coaching me."

"Coaching you? I bet!"

"Megan, take your mind out of the gutter! He's been a perfect gentleman."

"How disappointing for you! As it happens, I have a date myself tonight, with Jack."

Jaycee was pleased to hear it. "Good for you! Where are you going?"

"We're going to the Stromboli Inn for pizza and then a walk around the Glenmore Reservoir," Megan answered.

"Jaycee, I've decided to take it slow this time with Jack Henderson. I really like him," she said.

"I think he's a keeper, Megan," Jaycee said. "I don't know, there's something about him that makes him seem like a good guy to have around."

"I know, right? He's a typical cowboy and yet it seems like there's a lot more to him than we know."

"Well, have a great time, Megan. I'd better go."

Megan hugged her. "I'll come downstairs with you. I'm supposed to meet Jack in the lobby. We can compare notes tomorrow."

AT EIGHT O'CLOCK, Sergei drove up to the front door of the Marriott hotel in a car he had rented for the occasion. He cut a striking figure in a well-fitting dark blue suit and crisp white cotton shirt open at the neck. His hair was brushed back smoothly, making his black eyes and strong brows more prominent.

Drop-dead gorgeous, thought Jaycee as she stepped out from the lobby to meet him.

"Good evening, Miss McRae," Sergei said with an appraising glance. "You look lovely. Like a princess." Before opening the passenger door, he leaned forward, took her hand, and lifting it to his lips, kissed it in the grand Russian manner.

"Thank you, kind sir." Jaycee was moved by the courtly gesture and couldn't wait to let him see what she was hiding under her demure shawl.

Once Jaycee was settled, Sergei closed the passenger door and got in the driver's side.

"Now," he said, reaching across to caress the side of her face. "Take me on an adventure. I am ready."

So am I, thought Jaycee, *more ready than you know.*

She acted as navigator until they reached the Eau Claire Market complex and parked the car. Walking across the footbridge to Prince's Island, they made their way to the River Café and were ushered to their reserved table, where a chilled bottle of Moët & Chandon was waiting on ice.

"Champagne!" Sergei exclaimed. "This is special treat, not easy to get in Russia."

"Perhaps you would prefer vodka?" Jaycee teased.

"*Nyet,* this is perfect," he said as he held her chair and then took his place across from her.

Jaycee watched his reaction as she let her shawl drop onto the back of her chair, revealing her sexy dress.

Sergei caught his breath and exclaimed softly in Russian. "You… you are so beautiful, Jaycee."

Jaycee smiled at him. "Thank you. I'm so glad you approve."

A waiter came to pour the champagne as they read the menu.

"Bison!" Sergei said. "You can order bison here? I have heard of this animal. Now I feel I'm in the Wild West."

"Yes," Jaycee answered. "There are several bison ranches in Alberta. It's much like beef steak, but leaner. It's very good."

"Very Canadian," Sergei said.

"It is. Would you like to try it?"

The waiter was back. Jaycee indicated with a nod that Sergei would order the food.

"Good evening. We will have the bison steak, rare, with pan roasted potatoes and asparagus." Sergei said to the waiter, before picking up the wine list and handing it to Jaycee. "And the lady will choose the wine."

Jaycee loved the way he deferred to her. She reviewed the offerings and chose a French Syrah she had heard was a good pairing with bison. She handed the wine menu back to the waiter.

"Yes. Right away. Sir… Madame." The waiter took his leave.

Jaycee savored a long sip of her champagne and looked out the window where the Bow River wound, dark and silky, past the restaurant.

"We used to come here, our whole family, to Prince's Island for festivals," she said.

Sergei followed her gaze. "Festivals?"

"Yes, children's festivals, music festivals, plays. There is an open theater in the park."

"We have many festivals in Russia, also. When we were young, my father and mother would take us to St. Petersburg in the summer. There is a big festival with music and dancing. When we were older, we did exhibition riding there."

Jaycee turned back to face him. "I would love to visit Russia someday."

Sergei reached across the table and took her hand. "Maybe I'll show you my Russia someday."

Jaycee smiled. "I'd like that, Sergei."

Sergei tightened his grip on her hand.

"Jaycee, I must tell you that being with you, working together… it's been special for me."

His eyes held a deep tenderness that made her heart skip.

"It's the same for me, Sergei. You have been so good to me, a good friend." *Friend? You idiot, Jaycee!* She glanced down and felt herself blushing.

"I wish to be… more. More than a friend." Sergei was looking at her intently.

"I haven't been sure that you…" Jaycee looked up with eyes full of longing.

Sergei, meeting her gaze, brought her hand to his lips, kissed it, and placed her palm against his cheek.

"You can be sure, *zvyozdochka*."

"What does that mean?"

"It means my little star."

Jaycee's heart filled with joy. She finally knew what her soul had been longing for. He was sitting right across from her.

AFTER DESSERT, Jaycee paid the bill and suggested they take a walk through the park, as it was a warm night. They strolled along slowly, holding hands, before stopping on the footbridge. The surface of the river glimmered with the reflection of the city lights, and the stars twinkled in the clear night sky. Jaycee leaned against the rail, looking down and pulling her shawl closer around her shoulders.

"I love the river at night," she said quietly. She felt Sergei's arms circle her from behind. She turned to face him, leaning back against the railing. They gazed at each other for a moment before Sergei brought his lips down to meet hers.

CHAPTER 11

$\mathcal{U}$nder the same stars, Megan and Jack walked along the Glenmore Reservoir, holding hands.

"Don't you love the pizza at the Stromboli Inn?" Megan said. "I swear it's the best in town."

Jack looked down at the petite woman by his side.

"I'm glad you enjoyed it, Megan. I did, too."

Megan looked up at him. Jack was ruggedly good-looking, with a confidence and ease that she admired. She knew he travelled a lot as a professional calf roper, and she surprised herself by wondering whether he ever planned to settle down.

"Are you competing this year, Jack?"

"Of course. You?"

"Yes, and I think we have a good chance of being in the money this time."

"You and Monkeyshines, right?"

"Right."

"I'll be rooting for you."

She squeezed his hand. "Thanks. I'll be rooting for you, too."

"Megan?"

"Hmm?"

"Your friend, Jaycee, has been practicing with one of the Russians, right?"

Megan stopped walking and turned toward him.

"Yes, so what?" she said.

"Have you met the Russians?"

"I've talked to one or two of them. They seem nice, except for the woman who is with them. She's a bit of a bitch. Why?"

He looked serious. "Listen, Megan. Tell Jaycee to be careful not to get too involved with them."

"Whatever for?"

"Never mind, just tell her, okay? There's a lot more going on than she knows."

"What's going on? Can't you tell me?" Megan was mystified.

"Meg, it's best you don't know more than that. Talk to Jaycee. And keep away from the Russians yourself. Okay?"

"Okay."

Jack put his arms around her waist. "And now that we've gotten that out of the way, how would you feel about a kiss?"

Megan didn't answer, just stood on tiptoe and wrapped her arms around his neck, offering her lips to him.

ON THE BRIDGE in Prince's Island Park, Sergei and Jaycee clung to each other, their passion escalating. Sergei pulled the comb from the top of her head, releasing her waist-length hair. He twined his fingers in the luxurious tresses as she tightened her arms around his neck. She could feel him harden as he pressed closer, which only served to heighten her arousal.

"We need to go somewhere," Sergei said, breathing hard.

"Yes, I couldn't agree more," said Jaycee with a smile.

Sergei took her hand and led her quickly to the car. He drove like a man possessed until they arrived at the RV park. It was late and the park was dark and quiet. Instead of getting out, Sergei leaned across and kissed her, reaching down to push her dress up over her thighs. Taking his lead, she guided his hand between her legs. Sergei nuzzled her ear as his fingers found their way to the delicious wetness beneath her panties. She gave a gasp as he began to stroke her.

"Ohhh… Sergei…!"

She dropped her head back and closed her eyes. It was the most exquisite and pleasurable torture, and she wanted it to go on forever. The idea that a neighbor might see them made the intimacy even more forbidden and exciting. After a time, Jaycee reached down to unfasten his belt and unzip his pants. Sergei pulled off her lacy panties and dropped them to the floor of the car.

All she could think of now was having him inside her. She watched impatiently as he sat back in the driver's seat and took a small packet from his pocket. He slid the seat back to make room for her and pulled on the condom. Jaycee couldn't wait another second. She climbed on top of him and lowered herself down, taking his erect member in her hand and guiding him into her. Sergei groaned with pleasure as Jaycee began to move rhythmically up and down, her hips swaying, her hands gripping his shoulders. He fondled her breasts before closing his eyes and giving himself over to the pure bliss of her body moving on his. After a few minutes, Jaycee felt his fingers once again between her legs, driving her into new realms of pleasure. "Oh…yes, yeeessss…" She flung her head back, her long black hair brushing her back and her eyes closed as her fingers dug into his skin.

She could tell that Sergei was getting close. She began to move faster, moaning with ecstasy.

"Jaycee…!"

They climaxed together, crying out in unison.

A few minutes later, glowing with sweat and satisfaction, Jaycee rolled back into the passenger seat. Sergei turned to look at her, still caught in a daze of pleasure. She smiled impishly, rearranging her crushed dress down over her legs.

"Fast and furious!" she declared. His face broke into a wide smile.

"I think we should go inside now?" Sergei asked. They both laughed. She retrieved her panties and shoes from the floor as he pulled his pants up.

Just before they left the car, Sergei traced one finger down her moist face, pushing her wet hair from her eyes.

"We are good together," he said.

"*Da*," replied Jaycee.

CHAPTER 12

*T*he next afternoon, Jaycee was in the barn, getting Luna ready for practice. She was having trouble focusing. All she could think of were the amazing hours she had spent with Sergei in his RV. They had talked and made love until both of them had fallen asleep. They slept until noon the next day, despite Petr pounding on the door of the RV at eight in morning and demanding that Sergei come out. They pretended not to be there, giggling into each other's shoulders like naughty children. Finally, Petr gave up. Sergei made coffee and eggs before driving Jaycee back to her hotel. She was fatigued, but immensely happy. They had arranged to meet at the paddock in the afternoon for another coaching session. She couldn't wait to see him again.

"Let's go, Luna." She led her horse out to the paddock and began to ride.

After dropping Jaycee off, Sergei poured another cup of coffee and sat down to consider the situation. Jaycee was the most remarkable woman he had met in a long time, and sex with her had been spectacular.

Not only had she responded excitedly to his own lovemaking, she had insisted he lie back while she gave her full attention to pleasuring him. The night had passed too quickly. He could hardly bear to let her go this morning. He realized he had found something with her that he could not give up. Was that fair to Jaycee? She didn't yet know the problems he and his family were facing. This made solving Petr's dilemma more urgent. Tonight, he would talk to Vladimir.

His thoughts were interrupted by a strenuous pounding on the door of the RV.

"Sergei! Where are you?" He heard Petr's demanding voice.

He went to open the door and his father pushed past him. He could see that Petr was livid as he closed the door.

"Where have you been? You missed our meeting! We were discussing the routines."

"Sorry, Papa. I wasn't feeling too well this morning. I must have slept through my alarm."

Petr shook his head, and Sergei felt guilty. He hated lying to his father.

"Have you had a chance to talk to Vladimir?"

"Not yet, Papa. Tonight. I'm going to coach Jaycee this afternoon."

"Be careful not to get too involved with the girl, Sergei. We have enough to deal with at the moment."

Too late, thought Sergei. *I am totally involved.*

"I promised that I'd help her. I must keep my word."

"Fine, but don't forget about your responsibilities with the troupe." With that, Petr went out the door, calling over his shoulder, "I expect you tomorrow morning, at nine o'clock, for our next meeting."

"Yes, Papa."

～

THAT EVENING, Sergei knocked on Vladimir's hotel room door. He heard voices arguing inside, which stopped the moment he knocked. Vladimir opened the door.

"Yes?" His voice was impatient.

"Vlad, we need to talk."

Vladimir looked behind him, then opened the door wider. Sergei was surprised to see Irina sitting on a chair beside the table.

"Irina?"

"Sergei, I'm so glad you've come! Vladimir and I have been discussing some changes to the routines. You can help us."

Sergei looked at Vladimir. "Perhaps later. Irina, I need to speak to Vlad alone."

"Okay, as you wish." Irina stood up and walked past him, running her hand down his arm as she went by.

"See you later, *Seryozha*?" she cooed.

"Later."

The door shut behind her. Vladimir immediately got some glasses out.

"Vodka?"

"Thank you."

The two men sat at the table and toasted each other. Vladimir looked expectant.

Sergei found it hard to begin. "Papa has told me of his problem, and of your offer to help."

"I see."

"Is there no other way, Vlad? What you are proposing is both dangerous and illegal."

"Maybe Petr should have thought of that before he got in over his head."

Sergei felt a cold rage course through him, but said nothing.

"Look, Sergei. This plan will make all of us rich. Once Petr's debt is cleared, we only have to do deliveries for Mr. Gagarin. Our cut will be generous."

Sergei frowned. "And, I assume, you would be the boss."

"Yes, but Petr could still appear to be in charge."

And take the blame, and possibly be imprisoned, while you go free, Sergei thought.

"There must be another way. Can we sell part of the business, or raise the funds somehow?" Sergei asked.

Vladimir shook his head. "My friends are not patient people, Sergei. They will not wait any longer. You and your father must agree to their proposal, and soon."

"Let me talk to my father again."

"Don't take too long," Vlad warned. "My friends will be arriving tomorrow to hear your answer. Don't disappoint them. What is more important, the business or your lives? Take the offer."

Sergei rose slowly.

"We will talk again, Vlad. I need time to think."

"You have no time. You must accept."

Sergei stared at him silently and then turned, walking out of the room.

CHAPTER 13

The chartered jet landed at the Calgary International Airport the following afternoon. A summer thunderstorm had left the tarmac damp, but the rain had ceased. Vladimir Ivanovich was there to meet the flight. He stood by a rented limo and watched as the hatchway opened and three men descended the stairs. One was older and gray-haired and the other two younger. All were dressed in custom-tailored summer suits. The flight crew followed, carrying the bags. Vladimir opened the trunk of the limo and stepped forward to greet them.

"Vladimir." The gray-haired man extended his hand.

Vladimir shook it heartily. "Welcome to Canada, Mr. Gagarin."

Mr. Gagarin gestured toward his companions. "Let me introduce Andrei Dyatlov and Vasily Lobachevsky, my employees."

Vladimir shook their hands.

"Now, get in, Vlad. We'll talk."

Vasily opened the back door of the limo. Vladimir waited until Gagarin was seated before getting in beside him. Vasily followed and sat across from them, while Andrei took the passenger seat in front with the driver. Closing the privacy window, the driver headed out of the airport to the highway.

Vasily poured two vodkas from the bar and handed them to Gagarin and Vladimir.

"*Za zdorov'ye!*" The men raised their glasses, drank, and set them down on the bar counter. Vasily refilled their glasses immediately.

"Well?" Gagarin asked.

Vladimir knew what was expected. "I have talked to them. They know they have no choice. They hope, of course. But they must comply."

"We must have more than that. They must be willing. They must be able to keep their mouths shut."

"The father and older brother control the two younger ones. They will do as they are told."

"And Irina?"

"She is working on the older brother." Vladimir's tone gave him away.

"But?"

Vladimir hesitated.

"There is another woman he is seeing."

"Who?"

"A Canadian rider. Sergei has been coaching her."

"Has he told this woman anything?"

"I doubt it."

"But you don't know?"

Vladimir was silent.

"We will ask Sergei. If he has talked to her about our plans, you know what we must do."

MEGAN AND JAYCEE were in the barn, feeding the horses.

"Jaycee?"

"Yep?"

"I need to ask you something."

"Shoot."

"I know you like Sergei, but how involved are you?"

Jaycee hesitated. She had shared some information about her date, but had left out the more intimate details. She sat down on a bale.

"I like him a lot, Megan."

Megan frowned.

"You know when Jack and I were walking at the reservoir the other night? He seemed to know things about the Russians, but he wouldn't tell me what. He did ask me to tell you to be careful around them."

"Careful? Why?"

"Like I said, he didn't tell me anything, just asked me to warn you."

Jaycee didn't know what to make of this. A cold chill went through her. She knew little about the Volkovs, even though she was certain that she was falling in love with Sergei. *What had she gotten herself into? And what did Jack Henderson know?*

"That doesn't make sense, Megan. How does he know them, anyway? They only arrived here last week."

"Honestly, I don't know, but you can trust Jack."

"Megan, I need to process this. It may be a good idea for me to talk to Jack."

"Fair enough. He's coming by the hotel tonight for a drink. Meet us in the bar and I'll give you guys space to talk."

"Okay, Megan. Thanks. I won't keep him long. How's it going with the two of you?"

Megan grinned.

"Pretty darn good, thank you! We had a great time the other night. That's why we're meeting again. We might go out to a movie later."

"I'm glad, Megan. You deserve a good man."

"Do I? I've done a great job of screwing up my life to this point. Maybe this is my chance to be happy."

Jaycee got up and hugged her friend. "You're too hard on yourself. I'm sure this is a great chance for you, Meg. Keep doing what you're doing."

~

PETR AND SERGEI VOLKOV arrived at the door of Vladimir's room. He had left a message for them at the front desk.

Vladimir opened the door and invited them in. He was alone.

"Come in. Time to talk."

The three men sat together at the table.

"Vodka?"

Sergei and his father looked at each other.

"Not this time, Vlad. Say what you have to say."

Vladimir looked at them.

"The time has come. My friends are here from Russia. They must have an answer."

Petr looked at his son. "Sergei will speak for me," he said, folding his arms across his chest.

Sergei leaned forward. "We will meet with your friends. Then we will answer, but only to them."

Vladimir looked angry.

"I represent them."

"We'll speak only to them."

"Fine. I will arrange a meeting. They want to meet with you, too. But I warn you, be careful what you say."

Sergei nodded.

"Have you talked to the girl about our plans?" Vladimir asked.

Sergei looked puzzled. "Irina?"

"No, fool. The Canadian."

"Of course not." Sergei's temper flared. This was the first time Vladimir had spoken to him with such marked contempt.

"You're sure she knows nothing?"

"Nothing! I would never compromise her."

"Then end it with her. You have had your fun with her, now break it off, before Mr. Gagarin gets worried about her. Let someone else satisfy her needs."

Sergei, his face red, rose from the chair with both fists clenched. Petr put out a hand and stopped him.

"Sit down, Sergei."

Vladimir smirked. "You better listen to Papa."

It was Petr who was angry now. He pointed a finger at Vladimir. "You are not the boss yet, Vladimir. Not until we agree to terms with Mr. Gagarin."

Vladimir shrugged his shoulders and walked over to the fridge to pour himself another vodka.

"Whatever you say, Petr, but I don't suggest you set any conditions, unless you want the police to find your bodies in a field near the city. What's left of them."

Sergei stood up again. "Time for us to go, Papa."

"I'll contact you tonight about when Mr. Gagarin is ready to meet," Vladimir said. "Don't be late."

JAYCEE SIPPED ON HER MARTINI. She needed a little extra fortification for her meeting with Jack.

Megan detected her anxiety. "Don't worry, Jaycee. I'm sure Jack knows what he is doing."

Jaycee could only wonder why a professional calf roper knew so much about a traveling Russian troupe. Where on earth could he have met them before, and why did he mistrust them? It was crazy. Was Jack a xenophobe with a special fear of Russians? She'd always considered him a sensible guy, honest and straight-forward, which is why she thought he would be perfect for Megan.

Jack Henderson strode into the bar.

Megan's face lit up as soon as she saw him. "Jack, over here!" she called, waving her hand.

Jack took a seat and ordered a beer. The three chatted about the upcoming Stampede events for a while and then Megan excused herself, saying she had to go to her room to make a call.

As soon as she left, Jaycee turned toward Jack.

"All right, Jack, what is all this about Sergei Volkov and his family?"

Jack looked around. The bar was nearly empty. He leaned forward and spoke in a low voice.

"Jaycee, keep your voice down. All I can say is, these people are dangerous. You need to stop associating with them. I mean it."

"Jack, what are you talking about? I hate to break it to you, but Sergei and I have already gotten pretty close. We have a date to work together tomorrow morning."

"Break it."

Jaycee's brows knit together and her lips tightened.

"Who are you to demand that, Jack Henderson? What's your problem? You'd better start talking and I mean now!"

Jack's tone was still low. "Jaycee, please believe me."

Jaycee said nothing but finished her martini and ate the olive.

"Talk, Jack, or leave me alone. I'm not giving up Sergei."

Jack's reply was to take a small wallet out of his pocket and flip it open. It contained an RCMP badge and identification card. Jaycee examined it carefully.

"How do I know this is real?" she asked.

"Meet me at the Calgary headquarters tomorrow morning and they'll confirm it for you."

Jaycee was satisfied. "Are you undercover?"

"Yes."

"But you're a cowboy."

"Yes, that's right, I grew up on a ranch south of Calgary."

Jaycee was incredulous. "This is like something out of a movie."

"I know it seems that way, but the main points are these. Stay away from the Volkovs. And by the way, this conversation never happened. Megan knows nothing, including the fact that I'm a cop.

And just for now, I want to keep it that way. Jaycee, you know I care for her. I also care for you and your family. The less you know the better." Jack put away the badge and ID card, just as Megan exited the elevator and made her way to the bar.

Jaycee stopped the waitress as she passed by their table.

"Another round, please. For the three of us. And make mine a double."

PETR AND SERGEI were picked up by Gagarin's driver and taken to the penthouse suite of the Palliser Hotel. Vladimir was waiting for them in the lobby.

"This way," he said, leading them to the elevator. Exiting on the top floor, Sergei saw two burly young men, clearly Gagarin's bodyguards, stationed outside the door of the suite. On their orders, he and his father held out their arms to be patted down before entering.

Gagarin was seated on a sofa and looked up as they entered. He closed the book in his hand and laid it on a side table.

Rising, he extended his hand first to Petr, then to Sergei.

"Welcome, friends. Please be seated."

One of the bodyguards had followed them in. He went to the bar to fill a tray with glasses and a bottle of vodka, which he set down on the coffee table in front of them.

"I make a toast to our new venture," Gagarin said as he raised his glass. "*Za zdorov'ye!*

The men drank together. Gagarin put down his glass and rubbed his hands together.

"Now, let us begin. I think Vladimir has explained what is required?"

Petr and Sergei nodded.

Sergei said, "We sign over our business to you. You will pay my father's debts, and we will continue to work as a troupe, but with extra duties."

"You understand what those duties are?"

"We are to move drugs across borders in Europe and America under your direction."

Gagarin frowned. After a long pause, he turned to his bodyguard. "Vasily, you have patted them down? No wires?" The guard nodded.

Gagarin turned back to his guests. "Please, no need to be so specific, but yes, that is what you will do for me. And you have not discussed this with anyone?"

"No," Sergei said.

"Good. Very good. Vladimir, you have the papers drawn up?"

"Yes, Mr. Gagarin, I have them here."

Gagarin turned a critical eye on Petr and Sergei. "You understand that once you sign these papers, I am in control?"

"We do," Petr answered.

"And there is no going back?"

"We understand."

"Fine. Once you sign, the troupe will be mine and you will do as I say. Vladimir will be in charge and give you your next instructions. In the meantime, I will pay your debt to the casinos. Understood?"

Again, Petr and Sergei nodded.

"We need to hear you say it," Vladimir said, sneering at Sergei.

Sergei wanted to punch him. He and his father answered in unison. "Yes, Mr. Gagarin."

Without another word, Vladimir handed them a pen. Both men signed the bottom of the contract that would ruin their lives.

"One more thing," Gagarin said. "This Canadian woman, Sergei. She knows nothing of our plans?"

Sergei's blood ran cold but he kept his voice calm. "Nothing. You do not need to be concerned."

Gagarin smiled broadly. "Good. Good! We will drink, to seal the bargain."

Sergei felt like he was choking on the final glass of vodka.

Finally, the meeting was over.

On the ride back to their hotel, Petr looked like he had aged ten years. He stared bleakly out the window of the limo, his haggard face revealing his despair. Sergei rested his hand on his father's arm.

"We will be all right, Papa. We will survive this."

"Sergei, I'm so glad your mama is not here to witness my foolishness."

"She would understand. We'll work together as a family and try to do our best."

Petr turned and stared at him.

"Do our best? To be good criminals? No, Sergei, there is no 'best' in this situation." He turned his face away.

Sergei said nothing more, but left his hand on his father's arm.

THAT NIGHT in her hotel room, Jaycee expected to hear from Sergei to confirm their morning coaching session, but no call came. It was just as well; she had to think through what Jack had told her. Still a bit tipsy, she dialed the number of Sergei's RV and left a message.

"Sergei, it's Jaycee. I'm not feeling well. I won't be able to make our morning session. Okay? Talk to you soon. Thanks."

She put the phone back in the charger and sat on the bed to think. This was a disaster. The Volkovs must be in some sort of trouble, if Jack was so worried about her involvement with them. Then a thought occurred to her. Russia had its own mafia. Maybe some members of the Volkov family were involved?

Oh God. What have I gotten myself into? Have I endangered myself and my family?

The phone rang. Jaycee nearly jumped out of her skin before picking up the receiver.

"Sergei?"

"No dear, it's me."

"Mom?"

"We haven't seen you in a couple of days, honey. Just checking in."

Jaycee put her hand over the speaker, took a deep breath and composed herself.

"I've been busy, you know, Mom, practicing."

"Who is Sergei?"

"He's another trick rider who's been coaching me. We are supposed to meet tomorrow but I'm not feeling well."

"Is there anything I can do? Shall I come over? We're just down the hall."

"No, no, don't do that. I need to get into bed and sleep. I'm sure I'll be fine. I'm just tired."

"Well, okay honey, but don't hesitate to call us."

"I will if I get worse. Love you, Mom."

"Love you more. I'll check on you tomorrow."

"Okay, bye."

Jaycee hung up the phone, took a long hot shower and crawled into bed.

CHAPTER 14

*P*etr and Sergei knew the time had come to tell Mikhail and Dmitri of Petr's difficulties and their meetings with Vladimir and Gagarin. Both were dreading it. The two younger Volkov brothers sat expectantly in Petr's hotel room, assuming they were about to hear about changes to the routine for their next performance.

Petr looked at Sergei, then back to his younger sons, and began. "Mikhail, Dmitri, I have bad news."

The boys looked surprised and both glanced over at Sergei.

"Yes, Papa? Is everything all right?" Mikhail inquired.

"No, son. I'm in trouble, and I've brought you into trouble with me."

"What do you mean?" Dmitri asked.

There was no way to soften the blow.

"I owe money to the mafia in Russia. Gambling debts."

Mikhail and Dmitri sat stunned. Sergei could see them trying to process the information.

"What will you do?" Mikhail finally asked.

"I must give them control of the troupe."

"Give it to them! We can start another troupe, can't we, Papa?" Dmitri asked.

"You don't understand. They don't just want the business. They want us. They want us to smuggle drugs, Dmitri. We can't leave. We must do what they say or face the consequences."

Mikhail paled, but Dmitri was still in denial.

"What consequences?"

Mikhail turned to him. "Foolish boy! He means they'll kill us all if we don't do it."

Dmitri stared at Mikhail, then ran into the bathroom. They could hear him vomiting, then the water running. He returned to the room and dropped into a chair, his face completely drained of color.

Petr was miserable and contrite. "I'm sorry, Dmitri, Mikhail. So sorry."

"Listen, we must come to an agreement with each other," Sergei said. "There's no way out. We don't have the money to pay the debts, and the boss is here from Russia. We'll cooperate, at least for now. In the meantime, don't speak to anyone about this."

THE NEXT MORNING, Jaycee realized that she couldn't avoid going to the barns, even if she wanted to. She had promised Megan she would check on the horses and clean the stalls, so Megan could watch Jack compete in the calf roping. Still no word from Sergei. Jaycee wondered if he had received her message. Leading Luna and Monkey out of their stalls, she tied them nearby and picked up a pitchfork, hoping she could finish her chores before Sergei showed up.

"Jaycee."

Jaycee whirled around, still holding the pitchfork, which was now pointed in his direction. Her movement was so sudden that

Luna and Monkey shied away. It took a moment for her to realize how ridiculous she looked.

Sergei held his hands up and feigned fright. "Please don't hurt me!" he said in a falsetto voice. Then he laughed.

"That's not funny," Jaycee retorted, lowering the pitchfork and leaning it against the wall.

"You're right," Sergei said, smiling. He tried to reach for her, but she backed away. *Oh God, I'm afraid of him and he sees it.*

"What's wrong, Jaycee? Do you think I'll hurt you? I'd never do that, *zvyozdochka.*"

"I know. But Sergei, we need to talk about our relationship. Soon you'll be going back to Russia, and my life is here." She placed her hand on his arm. "To be honest, I'm having doubts."

Sergei took her face in his hands and looked deeply into her eyes. "You can feel it, *da*? That we have something special? What does your heart tell you?"

Jaycee's eyes welled up. "My heart tells me that we're good together. That I care deeply for you."

He pulled her into his arms and held her close. "I feel the same. There are some problems, but I need you to trust me, Jaycee."

SERGEI COULDN'T STOP THINKING about his conversation with Jaycee as he watched his brothers practice that afternoon. He knew he was falling in love with her. But should he have asked her to trust him when his own life was in such turmoil? When he was about to commit a crime?

He was still pondering these questions when he noticed a man about his own age standing by the fence. The man was leaning on the top rail, dressed in jeans, a plaid shirt, and a straw cowboy hat. He looked vaguely familiar. Sergei was used to having people stop by to watch them practice, especially here in Canada, so he didn't give the visitor a second thought. He was leading Pasha and Vadesh back to the barn when the man fell into step beside him. Dmitri and Mikhail had already headed in the opposite direction to get coffee.

"Sergei Volkov?"

"*Da*? Can I help you?"

"My name's Jack Henderson. I'm a friend of Jaycee McRae's."

Sergei stopped. He remembered where he'd seen this man before. At Ranchman's, dancing with Jaycee and her friend.

"Jaycee? Is she here?"

"No, it's you I want to talk to."

"Talk to me? Why?"

"I need to talk to you in private. Can you meet me at the midway tonight? Near the right side of the Main Stage at about seven?"

"Why can't we talk here?"

"Just meet me at seven o'clock near the Main Stage. Okay?"

Sergei was puzzled, but agreed to meet. He was curious to find out what this man wanted to discuss.

RUTH ELLIS WAS WORRIED about her daughter. She always knew when Jaycee was holding something back. Did she have feelings for this new man she had met, Sergei Volkov? Jaycee had recently introduced her parents to Sergei when they stopped by to watch her practice. He had seemed very nice to Ruth, and she could tell that he was falling hard for Jaycee. If Cody now had a rival, then maybe Jaycee was trying to choose between her two suitors?

"Ready, Ruth?" Ellis McRae was dressed in his best Western suit, his boots shining and his felt Stetson sitting on his head at a jaunty angle. "We should head out or we'll miss the reception."

They had been invited to a cattlemen's dinner at the Palliser Hotel. It was one of the events they enjoyed attending each year at the beginning of Stampede week.

"I'll be right with you, hon."

Ruth put on her gold earrings and picked up her silk stole.

"Ellis, I talked to Jaycee last night and I feel like something is bothering her. Something besides the riding."

Ellis took the stole and draped it around her shoulders.

"Should I talk to her?" he asked.

"Maybe." Ruth tucked her arm through his.

"Is it that Russian guy who's helping her?"

"How do you know about that?"

"Hey, I'm not blind, honey!"

Ruth chuckled and patted him on the arm. "Always the watchful father."

"Yes, and I've seen the way he looks at her. He's smitten."

"Of course," Ruth replied, smiling. "It's been like that with men since she was in high school."

"I'll talk to her."

"Thanks, Ellis. I appreciate it."

By SEVEN O'CLOCK, the midway at the Calgary Stampede was alive with the sound of people talking, laughing, and shouting. The smell of cotton candy, fried corn dogs and mini donuts drifted through the air. Ringing bells and shrilling whistles blared from the game booths. Screams of passengers on amusement rides echoed across the pavement. Amid the bedlam, Sergei found the right side of the Main Stage and stood, waiting for Jack's arrival.

Jack appeared almost immediately.

"Come with me, Sergei," he said, pointing to the nearby beer gardens. He directed Sergei to sit at a table near the tarp in the far corner, then went to the bar. Soon he was back with two large red plastic cups of draft beer.

"This is good beer. It's called Big Rock, and it's made right here in Alberta," Jack said. He raised his glass. "To new friends and new enterprises."

Sergei raised his glass and the men drank. The beer tasted wonderfully cool and refreshing in the heat and noise of the midway.

Jack leaned across the table. "Sergei, I need your help."

Sergei was both surprised and mystified. "*Da*, I will help if I can, but I don't understand…"

Jack looked around to make sure he wouldn't be heard. "I'm investigating Gagarin."

"Investigating?"

Jack took out his identification, as he had done with Jaycee, and showed it to Sergei.

"Sergei, I'm a detective with the RCMP. We've been following Gagarin for months now, here and in Russia. We know that Vladimir Ivanovich and Irina Petrov are working for him."

Sergei took a moment to think. He had always suspected Vladimir of duplicity, but he was surprised to hear about Irina. "You know about my father's troubles?"

Jack nodded. "We do. I suspect your father was forced to hire Ivanovich and Petrov. Sergei, I need to ask you something, and please answer truthfully. Is Gagarin planning to use your troupe to smuggle drugs?"

Sergei hesitated, but he was sure that Jack was sincere. On top of that, Jack was a friend of Jaycee's.

"*Da*," he said.

"Thank you, Sergei. I know this is all because of your father's debts. He's been left with no choice. That's how Gagarin does things. Am I correct?"

Sergei nodded. "Jack, I want to protect my family. Can you help?" he said, his eyes pleading.

Jack put his hand on Sergei's shoulder.

"I can help, but here's what I need you to do for me."

It was the start of the week-long rodeo performances at the Calgary Stampede. Jaycee was spending the morning practicing. Although she had followed Sergei's visualization technique, it had only helped to a certain extent. There were times when she was close to doing the Death Drag, but she still lost her nerve at the last minute. Jaycee knew she would never be truly confident until she had performed the trick successfully in front of a large audience. She had come to a decision. If she wasn't able to perform the Drag during the coming week, this would be her last Stampede and the end of her trick riding. She couldn't imagine what it would be like to stop performing, but she had to be realistic. The Stampede committee wouldn't be interested in a trick rider who was unable to perform the most crowd-pleasing stunt in any rider's repertoire. It would be humiliating, but she would survive.

Urging Luna into a gallop, she managed to complete a few tricks, but slowed to a canter when she saw Cody Phillips standing at the other end of the paddock. She reined Luna over to him and came to a stop.

Jaycee felt immense guilt at the sight of him. She and Cody had been seeing each other before the Stampede and she certainly hadn't anticipated getting involved with someone else. She knew Cody would be at the cattle auctions at some point, but she hadn't expected to see him during the Stampede because of his work on the ranch.

"Cody! What brings you here?" she asked, smiling. She was determined to act natural, despite her mixed feelings.

"Hi, Jaycee. Just wanted to see you, that's all." He patted Luna's neck. "You're lookin' good out there. How's the routine shaping up?"

"Pretty good. But not there yet."

"Well, I know you'll ace it. I can't be at your performance tomorrow because of the auction, but I'll be cheering you on from afar. Can I see you tomorrow night?" Cody reached up and squeezed her hand.

"Thanks, Cody, but I already promised a friend I would meet them afterwards. Rain check?"

"No problem. I'll be in touch again soon. Good luck today."

"Thanks, Cody. I appreciate it." Jaycee felt like a criminal as she reined Luna back into the paddock.

"READY TO GET SOME DINNER, JAYCEE?" Megan was rifling through her purse for her lipstick.

"Sure, give me a minute."

One thing Jaycee loved about Megan was that no matter what was happening in her love life, she always had time to do things with her girlfriends.

"Okay, I'm ready, Megan."

The two women were dressed casually. They had made a five o'clock reservation for dinner in the hotel café because they were tired and wanted to make an early night of it.

"How did the talk go with Jack?" Megan asked on the way down in the elevator.

"Fine. He was just being protective because Sergei is from out of town. He was worried I'd get hurt when he left."

"So there wasn't some deep dark secret? He was doing the big brother thing?"

"That's right."

Megan shook her head. "Why make such a big production out of it, then? I don't get it."

Jaycee wished she could tell Megan more. "Oh, you know how guys are. Forget about it."

They took the elevator to the lobby and entered the café, seating themselves at a table for two.

"Where are your parents tonight, Jaycee?"

"At a cattlemen's dinner at the Palliser. They go every year." Jaycee took a breath. "Megan, I saw Cody today."

"Cody? I thought you said he wouldn't be around for Stampede?"

"He was at the cattle auctions. He stopped by the paddock but we only talked for a short time."

"Does he know about Sergei?"

"Um, no." Jaycee felt a wave of guilt wash over her.

Megan frowned. "You're going to have to tell him at some point, Jaycee."

"I know. I'm just waiting for the right moment."

"Well, don't wait too long." Megan advised, then wisely let the subject drop.

As they waited for their appetizers, Jaycee noticed two young men come in and sit at a table nearby. They were dressed in formal summer suits and looked out of place among the other diners garbed in casual attire at this early hour. The men called the waiter over and Jaycee heard them order with a foreign accent. They sounded exactly like Sergei.

"Boy, you see all kinds during the Stampede," Megan remarked, following Jaycee's gaze. "Look at those guys. Who dresses like that at five o'clock? Spies?"

Jaycee's heart came into her mouth. She immediately turned her gaze back to the menu.

"What are you having?" Megan asked.

"Just a salad, I think. I'm not too hungry."

"Let's share a big Caesar salad then, and I'll order a steak."

"Sounds good." Jaycee tried to steal another look at the two men. To her dismay, they were both staring at her.

"Actually, Megan, I'm not feeling well. Do you mind if I skip dinner?"

"Oh Jaycee, I'm sorry, sweetie. Of course not. I'm okay on my own. Meet you upstairs?"

"Yes." Jaycee felt like she couldn't breathe. The men now seemed to be studying their own menus. Was she imagining things?

Watching to make sure she wasn't followed, Jaycee reached her room and put both locks on the door.

DESPITE HIS TROUBLES, Sergei felt confident the next day as the Volkov troupe prepared for their first performance. Irina was inspecting the entire troupe, making last-minute adjustments to the costumes and tack. The men were dressed in red satin shirts with black trim, flowing sleeves, and wide cuffs. Their loose black cossack pants and knee-high boots completed the effect. Irina was wearing the same pants and boots but her shirt was Prussian blue satin, designed to complement her fair complexion.

When all six members of the Volkov troupe galloped into the arena to the sound of recorded Russian folk music, the crowd went wild. With their traditional costumes, beautiful horses and vivid white, blue, and red Russian national flags, they made a memorable spectacle. Sergei, energized by the cheers and clapping, grinned at his brothers as they took their places for the first routine. He could even see some small Russian flags in the hands of the audience members. What followed was one of the best performances ever given by the Volkov troupe.

THAT NIGHT, the troupe gathered in Sergei's RV to celebrate their debut. The vodka and beer were flowing. Mikhail and Dmitri had picked up fried chicken and French fries as a treat for everyone.

Sergei lifted his beer to salute the troupe. "Well done! You all did a fine job today. I think I can say we are a success in Canada!"

"Are we?" Petr asked, his voice filled with bitterness. He was staring at the untouched plate of food in front of him.

"Yes, we are!" Irina said. "We have a big future ahead of us. Come on, Petr, enjoy yourself." She winked at Mikhail and downed another glass of vodka. She had squeezed herself in next to Sergei at the back of the table, making sure they were as physically close as possible.

For the rest of the evening, Sergei, Dmitri, and Mikhail tried to lighten Petr's mood, recounting funny stories and telling jokes, but their humor couldn't penetrate the heavy gloom that was emanating from their father. He was drinking more than usual and had not touched his food. Finally, Sergei whispered to Mikhail.

"Time to take Papa back to the hotel. He is tired."

"Yes, Sergei."

Petr was more than willing to go. He was clearly in no mood for celebration.

Vladimir spoke to Irina. "Do you need a ride back to the hotel?"

Irina shook her head and gave him a knowing look. "Sergei will drive me home, won't you, Sergei?"

Sergei absent-mindedly nodded his head, as he watched his father and brothers leave. Vladimir had said goodnight and was already gone before Sergei realized he was alone with Irina.

"Come on, Irina, I'll call you a taxi. I've had too much to drink to drive you home."

"Not yet, *Seryozha*, let's have one more drink before I go," Irina said.

Sergei was too drunk and too tired to argue with her.

"Okay. Just one." He poured them both another vodka.

"Sergei?" Irina put her hand on his chest and looked up at him. "Don't you like me even a little bit?"

Sergei looked at her with bleary eyes. "Of course I like you."

"Then kiss me, please? Just one little kiss to show me it's true."

Sergei stared at her for a moment and then took her face in his hands. He kissed her forcefully with all the despair, anger, and frustration he had in him. As soon as he let her go, Irina moved from behind the table and went over to sit on the sofa.

Sergei got up from the table and lurched unsteadily in her direction. He hadn't realized how drunk he was. As he reached the sofa, Irina grabbed his arms and pulled him down beside her. She began to unbuckle his belt, and Sergei immediately pushed her hands away.

"No. No, Irina!"

Irina put her hand on his knee. "It's okay, Sergei. I know what is worrying you. Vladimir told me. I can make you feel better."

Sergei turned and stared at her. "What? What do you mean?"

"*Seryozha*, I know who we are working for now. Mr. Gagarin. This is a good thing. Think of all we can do with the money we will make!"

"Are you mad, Irina? These people are dangerous. They may not even pay us. They are more likely to kill us."

"Of course they will pay us, Sergei. Mr. Gagarin is always good to his employees."

"And how do you know that?"

Irina realized she had made a mistake. "I…I heard it, from many people, back in Russia. If we make enough profits for Mr. Gagarin, we can have everything we want."

Sergei stood up.

"Time for you to go, Irina."

His tone was final.

CHAPTER 15

*T*he day Jaycee had been dreading finally arrived: her first performance at the Stampede. Sergei was there to help her prepare. Her parents were in the grandstand.

"Remember," he said, "your body knows what to do. Don't think too much."

"Yes, Sergei."

She patted Luna's neck as they waited in the entrance to the arena. "We can do this, Luna… that's my girl."

She turned to Sergei, who hugged her tight and kissed her forehead. "Enjoy your ride. I am here, *moya malen'kaya zvezdochka. Ya lyublyu tebya.*"

Whatever that means, I like the sound of it, Jaycee thought as she mounted Luna and the announcer began his spiel.

"Ladies and gentlemen, boys and girls, we have something special in store for you this afternoon! All our riders here at the Calgary Stampede are outstanding athletes, but this young lady adds something extra special to the fine art of horsemanship! Or should I say horse-womanship?"

The crowd laughed.

"Trick riding requires a special bond between horse and rider, and many years of training. Believe me, you are in for a treat! From Okotoks, Alberta, please welcome the incredible Miss Jaycee McRae and her horse, Luna!"

Resounding applause greeted Jaycee as she galloped into the arena, waving her hand and smiling. She was dressed in a green and aqua bodysuit trimmed with silver sequins and finished with shining silver cuffs. Her long raven hair, loose and flowing, was pushed back with a glittering silver hairband. Luna was perfectly groomed, her mane and coat shining beneath the blue and white leather tack and trick saddle. Jaycee could see her parents sitting with Megan in the front row.

After circling the arena, it was time to start her routine. She set Luna into a steady gallop. Within minutes she had performed Front and Back Fenders, a Stroud Layout and the Hippodrome Stand. The crowd responded enthusiastically. Next, she added some Touchdowns and a Back Bend, followed by a Shoulder Stand on the back of the saddle. The crowd was loving every minute of her performance, clapping and whistling after each trick.

The announcer stepped in.

"Isn't she great? Now, friends, we come to the most dangerous part of the routine. This is a trick called the Death Drag, and for good reason. Please hold your applause." The audience quieted down and leaned forward in their seats.

Here goes, Jaycee thought to herself. She urged Luna forward, wrapped the reins around the saddle horn and took a deep breath. With her right foot and leg secured by a strap over the top of the saddle, she began to drop backward, straightening her left leg upward and pointing her toe. As she continued to drop farther back and prepare for the final release of her hands downward, Kerrie's unconscious face, covered in blood and dirt, rose before her. Jaycee panicked. She immediately curled upward, reached to grip the horn and swung herself back into the saddle.

She had failed.

Her heart ached as Luna galloped on, but she knew she must

keep a smile on her face. Waving her hand, she saw the blank expressions of the crowd as they waited for something more. There was nothing more.

Just total humiliation.

The announcer knew his stuff and immediately was back on the microphone.

"Well, folks, it looks like we may have had some kind of technical difficulty here, but don't you want to give the little lady a big hand? Miss Jaycee McRae and Luna!"

The crowd responded with applause and whistles as Jaycee rode out of the arena.

Sergei was waiting for her. Immediately the forced smile disappeared as she reined Luna to a stop. She bent her head down until her face was in Luna's mane.

"Sergei...?" It was the plea of a small child.

"It's okay, Jaycee. Come down."

Jaycee's red-rimmed eyes were filled with tears. Sergei caught her as she dismounted and she patted Luna's neck. "Good girl, Luna. It's not your fault."

"It's not your fault either, Jaycee," Sergei said. "You did your best and that's enough."

Without another word, he took the reins, put his arm around Jaycee's shoulder and walked her out, Luna following behind.

VLADIMIR AND IRINA were arguing in Vladimir's hotel room.

"What do you mean, you think Sergei knows you have been working for Gagarin?"

Vladimir was furious. "You were supposed to seduce him and keep him under control! Can't you do anything right?" he asked.

"Vladimir...I let something slip. I didn't mean to. I'm sorry, my love," Irina explained regretfully. "Sergei didn't say anything, but I could tell he suspected I had been lying to him about how well I knew Mr. Gagarin."

Vladimir banged his fist on the table. "Does Sergei know about us? That we're lovers?"

"No, I'm sure of that. I almost had him last night, Vlad. Sergei was drunk and we kissed, but then he wouldn't go further. He made me take a taxi home."

Vladimir slapped her across the face. "You stupid cow! You're going to have to keep working on him. The father and brothers do everything he says. If we have him, we have control over the whole family. Do you understand?"

Irina put her hand up to her reddened cheek. "I'll try again. I'm so close. Please, Vlad!"

"Mr. Gagarin will ask me about it and what will I tell him?"

"Tell him Irina Petrov knows how to control a man."

Vladimir smirked. "You don't control me."

Irina wrapped her arms around his neck. "That's why I love you, Vlad. You're strong and I feel safe with you."

Vladimir was used to Irina's flattery.

"Just do what I asked. Get Sergei in bed," he said.

"I will, my love, I will."

MEGAN DECIDED that Jaycee needed a distraction after her humiliating experience in the arena the day before, so she convinced her friend to return to Ranchman's for a night of drinking and dancing. After the women had found a table, Jaycee heard a familiar voice.

"Hello ladies. Can I buy you a drink?" Cody Phillips was standing by the table.

"Cody! What are you doing here?" Jaycee said as he took the seat beside her.

"Enjoying the Stampede of course! I decided to get a hotel room for a couple of days. A friend is looking after my ranch."

"Hey, Cody." Megan smiled. "If you're buying, I'll have a vodka tonic, thanks."

Jaycee held up two fingers.

"Two vodka tonics it is!" he said, winking at Jaycee as he headed for the bar.

Megan turned to Jaycee. "Don't tell him about Sergei yet, Jaycee," she said. "Just have some fun tonight and you'll feel better about what happened in the arena."

"I wish I could believe that," Jaycee answered, looking downcast.

"Well, forget about it, at least for tonight, and let yourself go. That's why we came."

Cody returned with the drinks. Megan caught his attention and tilted her head in Jaycee's direction, a subtle signal that Cody should ask her to dance. He picked up on it immediately.

"Dance, Jaycee?"

"Sure, I'd love to."

On the dance floor, Cody twirled Jaycee around twice and then took her into his arms. They had danced together so often in the past that they had their own style. They moved together flawlessly. The band was playing a song that Jaycee loved. They two-stepped their way around the floor, enjoying every minute and laughing as they went.

This is fun, Jaycee thought. *Megan is right.*

"How did the performance go?" Cody asked.

"Fine, just fine."

"And your parents? How are they?"

"They're good. Doing their usual Stampede activities."

"Glad to hear it."

Cody looked down at her with shining eyes and she suddenly felt uneasy. Cody had been part of her life since childhood. She loved him dearly and treasured the memories they had together.

But her feelings were entirely different when it came to Sergei Volkov. Her heart almost leapt out of her chest every time she set eyes on him. His muscular body, dark hair and penetrating eyes made her knees weak. When Sergei touched her, her bones melted. When he kissed her, she forgot everything but her urgent desire for him.

Cody was asking her something.

"You know how I feel about you, Jaycee, don't you?"

Jaycee met his eyes. "Yes… I think I do, Cody."

"I'm trying to fix up the ranch and build a good herd of Herefords. I need a good woman to help me."

Jaycee knew what was coming.

"I've loved you since I was a kid, Jaycee. We're good together and I believe we could be happy if we got married. Will you think about it?"

It was not how she had pictured her first proposal. She had hoped for something far more romantic, but this was so typical of Cody, always no-nonsense and straight to the point. She thought about what he was offering. Marriage, a home, a couple of kids, a simple life with a good man. She had once been very much in love with him. As she looked into his eyes, she saw how sincere he was and felt a surge of affection for him. With Cody, she would have a pleasant life, she knew that. And right now, she was at an all-time low. His offer was tempting.

Before she could answer, she saw Sergei across the floor, dancing with Irina. Her chest tightened and she felt cold all over. Cody saw the change in her expression and followed her gaze to the other couple.

"Who are they?" he asked.

"No one, Cody."

Sergei had seen her. He immediately stopped dancing and led Irina off the dance floor. *He wants to avoid me*, Jaycee thought. *Why? Because I failed after all his coaching? And what's he doing here with Irina?*

She felt dizzy.

"Cody, I need some air," she said urgently.

"Sure, honey." Cody led her toward the front door of the club and opened it for her. He followed as she walked outside. A large crowd was gathered by the outside stage, laughing and talking.

"I'll be fine, Cody. Give me a minute. Go back to Megan, I'll come in soon."

"Are you sure?"

"I'm sure."

Cody didn't argue. "See you inside, then. I'll order you another drink."

Jaycee nodded and walked across the street to distance herself from the noise and crowd. She found a small cement barrier next to a parking lot and sat down, staring at the ground with her arms wrapped tightly around her even though it was a warm night.

What am I doing? she thought. *Cody is a standout guy, sweet, good-looking and he's known me all my life. With Sergei, it's totally exciting and the sex is amazing, but I hardly know him. With the two of us living so far apart and being from different cultures, what kind of future can we have?*

Within minutes, Sergei was standing in front of her.

"Jaycee?"

Jaycee looked up, her face full of misery.

"Are you all right?"

"I'm fine. I just didn't know you'd be here."

He sat down on the barrier beside her.

"Irina asked me to come. My brothers are here, too."

"I see."

He took one of her hands. "Jaycee, are you unhappy about the performance? Please don't be. Everything will be all right."

Jaycee didn't know what perverse impulse made her ask. "And Irina? Are things all right with her?"

She could see Sergei was taken aback. "Irina? What do you

mean? Every day, every night, I think only of you, *zvyozdochka.* Irina is nothing to me."

Jaycee pulled her hand away and stood up. "Sergei, I'm sorry but I'm confused. I just don't see how we can make it work between the two of us, even if we want to be together. Our lives are too different. I need to make some important decisions about my future, so I'm asking you to give me some space."

Sergei stood up, a look of distress on his face. "Jaycee, please. Don't give up on us."

"I'm sorry, Sergei. I have to go. Someone is waiting for me."

It took everything she had to pull away from him. Giving him one last look, she turned and walked away.

CHAPTER 16

*S*ergei was in his RV, trying to sort out the events of the past few days. Since the night of the party, Irina had been following him around like a puppy and pushing him to spend more time with her. It was driving him crazy, but he promised Jack he would keep an eye on her. When Irina insisted they go dancing at Ranchman's, he invited Mikhail and Dmitri to avoid being alone with her. What he hadn't expected was to see Jaycee dancing with a handsome cowboy and obviously enjoying herself. He had felt a flash of jealousy. Then Jaycee saw him, and he could tell from her expression that she was equally unhappy to see him dancing with Irina. He wasted no time getting Irina off the dance floor. A few minutes later he saw Jaycee and her dance partner going out the front door of the club. He felt compelled to follow. Once outside, he found Jaycee sitting alone, across the street. He was glad to see that the cowboy was nowhere in sight.

He knew she was feeling depressed after her first performance. He felt distraught when she spoke about needing space away from him. But as a man of honor, there was no question that he would give her what she asked for. Her words sounded so final.

Yet he wasn't about to give up. He must fight to keep their love alive.

~

THE VOLKOV TROUPE's performances had been going well. Sergei and his brothers, as well as Vladimir, were getting a lot of attention from the female fans. Sergei kept aloof, but Dmitri, Mikhail and Vladimir were clearly loving it.

He talked seriously with his brothers about not getting involved with the women fans because of the situation they were in. Mr. Gagarin might see short-term girlfriends as "loose ends" to be taken care of before returning to Russia.

Mr. Gagarin and his bodyguards attended each performance, sitting in a box at the edge of the arena where Sergei and the troupe could see them. There had been several discussions in Mr. Gagarin's room about what they would be bringing back to Europe from North America. The Volkovs' part in Gagarin's criminal operation had already begun. And Sergei knew that worse was to come.

~

A FEW DAYS LATER, Ellis and Ruth McRae joined Jaycee in the hotel café for breakfast.

"Hi, sweetheart." Ellis leaned over to kiss his daughter on the head.

"Megan will be here soon, and Cody is joining us as well."

Ruth clapped her hands. "Cody? That's great!" She exchanged glances with her husband.

"Yes, he's here for the cattle auctions," Jaycee explained. "He… well, we've been spending quite a bit of time together these last few days."

"Oh Jaycee, I'm glad to hear it," Ruth said.

Ellis poured some coffee for all of them from the carafe in the middle of the table. "You perform again this afternoon, don't you?"

"That's right."

"You'll be fine," Ellis said.

"I know I will be, Dad."

Megan arrived and shortly afterward Cody came in and took the seat next to Jaycee. The waitress wrote down their breakfast orders. As they waited, they talked about the Stampede events they had been attending.

"Monkey and I are in the top run for the barrel racing," Megan shared. "I am so pumped!"

"That's wonderful, Megan dear. We are so proud of you," Ruth said.

Cody caught Jaycee's eye and she nodded to him.

"Mrs. McRae, Megan...Jaycee and I have something to tell you."

Ruth and Megan gave Jaycee and Cody their full attention. "I had a word with Mr. McRae earlier today. I'm proud to say he has given me permission to ask for Jaycee's hand in marriage, and Jaycee has agreed."

Immediately Ruth and Megan got up to embrace the couple.

"We are so happy for you both," Ruth said. She turned to Ellis and playfully slapped his hand. "Shame on you for keeping this from me!"

Ellis shook Cody's hand. "Well done, son."

"Congratulations, you two!" Megan exclaimed. "Can I be a bridesmaid? When's the big day?"

"Of course you can," Jaycee answered, smiling. "Who else would I ask?"

"We plan to be married next year," Cody explained. "We won't be able to honeymoon until I get the ranch back in shape, but I promised her I'd make up for it."

He put his arm around Jaycee.

Jaycee looked down to avoid catching her father's eye. "Of

course, I'll be giving up trick riding. I'll need to help Cody on the ranch."

Ellis looked surprized. "But you love riding, Jaycee. I know the last year has been hard, but you'll still want to perform, won't you?"

"No, Dad, I've made up my mind. The end of the week will be my last performance."

~

JACK HENDERSON MET Megan at a coffee bar at the Stampede grounds the next day.

"Jack, I've got awesome news! Jaycee is engaged to her high school sweetheart! And I'm going to be a bridesmaid!" Megan was lit up with excitement.

"Really? That's great!" Jack said.

"I'm going to be busy this year, helping her to get ready. I'm so happy for her!" Megan burbled on with more details as Jack sipped his coffee.

They had been seeing each other every day, and Jack had never been happier. His feelings for Megan had grown, and she seemed to be as delighted with the relationship as he was. He hoped she wouldn't change her mind about dating him once she found out he was a detective. Dating cops didn't sit well with some women. He had decided that as soon as his current case was resolved, he would tell Megan the truth. For now, it was best for both of them to keep that information under wraps. He didn't believe in relationships starting with a lie, but his public duty came first.

"I'm in the final round of the barrel racing on Friday. Will you come and watch me?" Megan asked.

"Wouldn't miss it," Jack assured her, reaching out to take her hand across the table. She beamed at him and he realized how much he loved that smile. Megan was a bit wild, but he knew how kind-hearted and sincere she was. He cherished her zest for life. He'd known the first time he'd seen her last year that this was the woman for him. Back then, she had broken his heart, unable to focus on only one relationship, but she seemed to have settled down.

Now Jack was ready to risk his heart a second time.

SERGEI AND IRINA were in the barn with the veterinarian, watching her check the horses for any minor injuries. He couldn't believe the Stampede was almost over, and that this afternoon would be their last performance. Soon they would be leaving for Russia. Irina led two of the horses back into their stalls, making sure they had enough feed. Then she rejoined Sergei, watching as the vet continued her work.

"So, I hear your little Canadian friend is getting married."

It was like a lightning bolt through Sergei's heart.

"What? What do you mean?"

"I heard some of the cowboys talking. Her boyfriend is here buying cattle, and they're planning to marry next year. Good for them, right?"

Sergei's mind raced. *Was Jaycee's fiancé the handsome cowboy he had seen dancing with her at the club? Why hadn't she said anything about it? How long had they been engaged?*

Vladimir came into the barn. "Sergei, Mr. Gagarin needs to see you."

PETR, Sergei, and Vladimir listened attentively as Mr. Gagarin instructed them to meet him in the barn after their final performance to receive the drugs they would be delivering to Russia. Getting the drugs past Canadian customs would be the greatest risk they would face. Gagarin explained that his people had been using a new type of strong non-permeable plastic that, if sealed correctly, could fool the sniffer dogs. The sealed packages would be sewn inside the tack and hidden in false bottoms Vladimir had built into the equipment trunks. Russian customs officials had already been bribed, so there would be no problem on the other side of the Atlantic.

"So, we are ready?" Gagarin asked.

"We're ready," Sergei answered.

"Good!"

"And if we're discovered at customs?" Sergei asked.

"You're on your own. You must have known that?"

Petr and Sergei looked at each other, then back at Gagarin.

"We know," Petr answered.

"Everything will go smoothly, boss," Vladimir added.

"When you get back to Russia, you'll be amply rewarded," Gagarin continued. "How would you like your own stables, arena, and riding school? That can easily be arranged. Then we'll hire more employees to help us with our projects."

Just what I've always wanted, Sergei thought. *A criminal enterprise bought with drug money.*

"We'll see," said Petr. "First we must get home."

"Of course." Gagarin smiled.

JAYCEE CONTINUED to perform but left the Death Drag out of her routine. Instead, she had added a few extra stunts and let the announcers know about the changes.

Honestly, she simply didn't care anymore. About any of it.

She knew she should be happy about her engagement to Cody, but every morning she found herself numb and depressed, dragging herself through the day with a fake smile pasted on her face. She had managed to fool Cody, Megan and her mom, but she could see her dad wasn't buying her act. She had caught him looking at her a few times with a worried expression.

Try as she might, she couldn't get Sergei out of her mind or her heart. She knew the Volkovs had their final performance this afternoon and would be preparing to return to Russia. She still hadn't told Sergei about her engagement, and soon she would have to say goodbye to him forever. The thought was agonizing.

Cody had been so busy with the cattle auctions that she'd barely seen him since they announced their engagement. She consoled herself with the thought that once the Stampede had ended, everything would go back to normal. She would marry Cody, be busy on the ranch, have a bunch of kids, and live happy ever after. She would forget Sergei.

Or so she told herself.

CHAPTER 17

The ambassadorial side of the Volkovs' visit to the Calgary Stampede was a complete success. The troupe had been interviewed by several television and radio stations in Calgary, and the Stampede Board had already invited them back for a second year. They continued to receive requests to perform in venues all across North America. The Russian government had sent their congratulations and were planning a large event in Moscow to welcome them home.

Now the time had come for their last performance. Over the past week, they had built a loyal following of fans. The crowd cheered wildly as they rode in and watched spellbound as they presented the most popular stunts in their routine: the tandem Shoulder Stands and Touchdowns, the three-man Hippodrome Pyramid and of course the Death Drag.

Sergei should have been enjoying all this success as he galloped around the arena smiling and waving to the crowd, but all he could think about was the upcoming meeting in the barn with Gagarin. He had reviewed everything he had been instructed to do. Word had finally come from Russia that all Petr's gambling debts had been paid, so that at least was something to feel good about.

Everything must go well this afternoon, Sergei thought. *I have to keep my nerve.* He thought of his mother and said a little prayer for God to be with the family in this dangerous time.

LATER THAT AFTERNOON, Mr. Gagarin and his bodyguards arrived at the barn. Andrei was carrying a large black duffle bag. Petr, Sergei, Vladimir and Irina were waiting for them. Sergei had sent Dmitri and Mikhail to the Fairfield Inn to finish packing the family's belongings. The horses had been transferred to a government veterinary facility, where the vet would inspect them and fill out the paperwork required for travel to Russia.

"Good afternoon, my friends. Is everything prepared?" Gagarin asked.

"Yes, boss," Vladimir said. "Please sit down." He gestured toward a chair and table he had brought from the barn office. Gagarin sat down and nodded to Andrei, who placed the black duffle bag on the table and unzipped it. Taped plastic packages, carefully sized and weighed, were inside.

"What you see here is worth a great deal of money," Gagarin said, his face grim. "Take good care of it or you will answer to me."

"I have the tack ready, Mr. Gagarin," said Irina. "All I have to do is sew the packages inside."

She is completely at ease, Sergei thought. *She's done this before.*

"Good work, Irina." Gagarin said, then continued his instructions. "Once you arrive in Moscow, you will be met by Mr. Rostovich and his colleagues. They will direct you to a private facility where the delivery will be completed. Then you must go home and wait for us to contact you."

"We understand," Sergei answered. "We are ready to go ahead."

Suddenly, Sergei turned and grabbed Petr by the arm, dragging him into an adjacent stall and pushing him to the floor behind some bales. He then threw himself down beside his father.

For a moment, Gagarin and his men simply stared at them, incredulous. Irina barely had time to glance at Vladimir before a group of men in black uniforms and helmets, holding assault weapons, swarmed into the barn. Andrei pushed Gagarin to the floor and kneeled over him as Vasily pulled out a pistol and started firing. Vasily was immediately shot in the thigh and went down. Gagarin and Andrei put their hands in the air as Vladimir and Irina were seized and handcuffed. An EMT crew came in to bind Vasily's leg and took him away. Gagarin, Andrei, Vladimir and Irina were bundled into a black van and removed from the scene. The last thing Sergei heard was Irina screaming curses and kicking the wall of the van.

As the response team began making their way outside, taking the duffle bag with them, the man who had been shouting orders during the raid stepped forward and pulled off his helmet. "Sergei, are you all right? It's safe to come out."

In the back of the stall, Sergei got up and helped Petr to his feet.

"We're fine, Jack," Sergei answered.

Petr was stunned, still trying to understand what had happened.

"Mr. Volkov?" Jack asked.

"*Da*…yes, I'm fine." Petr looked at Sergei questioningly.

"Papa, this is Jack Henderson. He is with the Royal Canadian Mounted Police. They have been investigating Mr. Gagarin and his group for some time, in relation to the drug smuggling. I could not say anything to you or the boys about this. It had to be secret."

Petr dropped into the chair recently occupied by Mr. Gagarin, and looked up at Sergei.

"What will happen now?"

Sergei put his hand on his father's shoulder. "We'll need to go with Jack and answer some questions."

"What about your brothers?"

"They're fine, Papa. They are with some officers at the hotel and will meet us at police headquarters."

Sergei knelt down beside his father. "Papa, you don't need to worry anymore. It's over. Your debts are paid. Gagarin is in custody."

Jack looked outside and signaled to Sergei that the police car was ready for them.

"Come, Papa. We can talk more at the headquarters," Sergei said.

Confused, Petr said, "Who will take care of the horses?"

"Don't worry about that, Papa. Jack's friends will take care of them. Let's go."

Jack Henderson led the way to the car.

CHAPTER 18

"*I* think it's about time I took my girl to lunch," Ellis McRae said to Jaycee as they put away the tack after Jaycee's final practice. Jaycee hung up the bridle and turned back to her father.

"Sure, Daddy, that would be fine. I should go clean up first."

She wasn't looking her best, Ellis noted. She was pale, and he could see that she hadn't even washed her hair, something she usually took great pride in.

"Jump in the car, honey. I'll take you back to the hotel, you can take a shower and then meet me downstairs in the café."

Ellis looked over at his daughter. Usually, when they drove anywhere together, she would chatter to him in a companionable way. Today she was silent, staring out the window.

He dropped her at the entrance to the hotel and went to park the car. Entering the hotel room, he saw Ruth reading on the bed. She looked up. He didn't need to say a word.

"Jaycee?" Ruth asked.

Ellis sat down and stroked his wife's leg. "It's bad, Ruth. I've never seen her like this. It's not just the riding."

"I know."

"She's pining."

"Yes, and I think I know why. Sergei."

"Has Cody said anything?"

Ruth put her book down. "I don't think he knows. Cody has been at the auctions every day, and Jaycee is often asleep by the time he stops by the hotel."

"I brought her home from practice. I told her I'd meet her downstairs for lunch."

Ruth reached out and took her husband's hand. "I don't know how to help her, Ellis. I think she has to work this out by herself."

Ellis sighed. "At least she knows we are here for her." He leaned over and kissed his wife, then got up and went to meet Jaycee.

In the café, Jaycee took another sip of water and moved her fork around on her plate.

"More water, honey?" Ellis was holding the water carafe over her glass.

"Sure, Dad, thanks."

"The practice seemed to go well today."

"Yes." Her voice was subdued.

They discussed the Stampede events of the last week. Ellis could see that Jaycee was only half-listening to him. He leaned forward and tapped his finger on the table. "Okay, Jaycee, that's enough."

Jaycee looked up, surprised. "Enough what, Dad?"

"That's enough of feeling sorry for yourself. I didn't raise you to mope around and be a quitter."

Jaycee put down her fork.

"Did I?" Ellis's tone was emphatic.

"No, Dad."

"Then smarten up. It's always about choice, Jaycee. You know that. You have to decide what you want. And then do everything you can to get it. I can see you're unhappy. Is it Sergei Volkov?"

Jaycee was in tears. "Dad, I've made a big mistake. I love Sergei and now I think I've lost him. And I've been so unfair to Cody."

"Well, be responsible and tell Cody the truth. He won't like it, but both of you will be better off. Then go after what you want, and your mother and I will back you one hundred percent. And above all, don't let circumstances dictate the life you will live. You are in charge. Understand?"

Jaycee got up, went around to his chair and hugged him.

"Dad, I have something I need to do." She looked resolute and determined.

"Well, go then! Don't sit around here with an old man like me!"

"I love you, Dad."

"Yep, I know."

Jaycee ran from the café.

CHAPTER 19

*A*fter giving their statements, and having a final word with Jack, the Volkovs were ready to go back to their hotel.

Jack took Sergei aside.

"We still have to determine whether you and your father will be charged for conspiring with the Gagarin group. We know you were being extorted, so that will work in your favor. So will your cooperation in ensuring the success of our operation. We've been trying to shut down the Gagarin group for years. We couldn't have caught them without your help. We've already arrested Rostovich and the rest of Gagarin's people over in Russia, and as it turns out, the group your father owed money to is not connected to Gagarin. In fact, they'll be pleased that they don't have to share the market anymore. Now that Petr's debt has been paid, he should have no more problems with the casino owners. We've also contacted the Russian government. They're aware that there will be a delay in your return home, but we haven't shared the other details of your situation with them. Okay? So, take it easy for now and I'll be in touch at the end of the week."

He held out his hand and Sergei shook it vigorously. "I don't know how to thank you, Jack."

"Thank me by enjoying the rest of your visit to Canada. I hear Jaycee's final performance is coming up tomorrow. See you there."

CHAPTER 20

"Cody, can we talk?" Jaycee was standing in the door of Cody's hotel room.

"Sure, come in. I'm glad to see you." Jaycee followed him into the room and sat down on the love seat.

"Beer?" Cody asked.

"Sure, thanks."

He fetched two cold beers out of the mini fridge and sat down beside her. "What's up?"

Jaycee took a breath. "Cody, you know I love you dearly. You've been a big part of my life and I would never want to hurt you."

He laughed. "Well, that's good, isn't it? I love you, too, Jaycee. I always have. That's why I can't wait for us to be married. I have some big plans for us. You know that line of Herefords I was looking at the other day? Well, I…"

Jaycee placed her finger against his lips. "Wait. I have something to say. I need you to listen, and I need you to understand, if you can."

Cody's face fell. "What is it? Are you sick? Are your parents okay?"

"We're all fine."

"Then tell me."

Jaycee took his beer out of his hand and put it on the coffee table with her own.

"Cody, I'm so sorry. I can't marry you."

He looked at her blankly. "What?"

"I love you, but I don't love you in the way that I should, the way you deserve."

"What do you mean?"

"I'm not in love with you. That's no way to start a marriage. Things might go smoothly at first, but eventually I know we'd be unhappy."

He shook his head. "No, Jaycee. We're perfect for each other. We know each other so well."

"That's exactly it. I know what you want, and I can't give it to you. It wouldn't be fair. Please try to understand."

Jaycee got up and walked to the door. She turned back toward him, her hand on the doorknob.

"I'm sorry. Goodbye, Cody."

$\mathcal{T}$he Volkovs were in their hotel room, sharing a much-needed round of vodka.

"But I don't understand, Sergei. How did the police know when to come?" Petr asked.

"Jack and I met up earlier this week on the midway," Sergei explained. "He told me who he was and what he was trying to do. He asked if I would help, and I said I would. He knew that Gagarin was using us to move the drugs. Today, when I said the words 'we are ready to go ahead', it was the signal for the Emergency Response Team to move in and make the arrests. I arranged ahead of time that Dmitri and Mikhail be at the hotel, and the horses at the vet facility when the raid went down. I knew it was important for both of us to meet Gagarin, Papa, to avoid suspicion. Jack told me to get you out of the line of fire as soon as I gave the signal. So, that's what I did."

Petr shook his head. "You are a brave boy."

"I did what I had to do."

"And now everything is as it was!" Dmitri lifted his glass. "Here's to our papa and our big brother. *Za zdorov'ye!*"

Everyone raised their glasses. After they drank, Sergei spoke again. "We a lot to celebrate, Dmitri, but not everything is settled. We need to wait to see if charges will be laid against us. Jack will let us know. And there's something else. I am not going back to Russia. I have asked to stay here, and Jack is going to help me in any way he can."

Petr was dismayed. "My son, why would you do that? How will the troupe continue without you?"

"You'll be fine. Mikhail and Dmitri are ready to help you run the troupe. Hire some new riders back home and train them. Remember, you'll be at the Stampede next year. The Russian government will send you back, and I will see you then. Papa, there is great opportunity to be had here. I want to start my own riding academy, a different kind of school with both Western and Eastern riding styles. And…I have…other reasons for staying."

Mikhail laughed. "Would one of those reasons have long dark hair and a pretty face? Do you think we didn't know you were falling in love? We saw how you looked at Jaycee when she came to our practices, and the two of you were always going off for coffee or lunch afterwards. Give us some credit, Sergei!"

Petr put his hand on Sergei's shoulder. "Son, you and Jack have given me back my freedom. Now I'll give you yours. You know I always wanted you to marry a Russian woman, but if you have found love here, then I'm glad for you. Your mother showed me that finding a good woman is the best fortune a man can have. She was proud of you, Sergei. Go ahead and make your plans. The boys and I will manage."

Sergei hugged his father. "Thank you for understanding, Papa."

Petr smiled.

"So, my boy, what are you still doing here? Go to her!"

CHAPTER 22

"Jaycee, let me help you with that."

Megan fastened the last snap on Jaycee's costume before twirling her around and surveying the effect. They were in the hotel room, preparing for Jaycee's final performance the following day.

"Wow."

Jaycee grinned at her. "So, it meets with your approval?"

"It does. That color really suits you. You look gorgeous." The costume was a deep rose color with gold metallic trim.

"So, where do you go from here, Jaycee?"

Jaycee had told Megan about her talk with her father, and her break-up with Cody.

"I'm going to keep riding, and Megan, I'm going to keep working on the routine until I can do everything I used to do."

Megan hugged her. "Good for you, girlfriend!"

"And you, Megan? What about you?"

Megan laughed. "Well, first of all, I'm planning to win the barrel racing. I'm that close and I know Monkey and I can do it. After that, I'm going to spend as much time with Jack Henderson as humanly possible."

"You really like him, don't you?" Jaycee asked.

Megan looked at her with shining eyes. "I love him, Jaycee. This last week with him has been…well, let's just say I'm happier than I've been in years."

Jaycee's eyes misted up. "I'm so glad, Megan. I'm sorry I haven't been myself lately. I feel I've let you and my parents down, and I've hurt Cody badly."

"You've been through a lot in the last few weeks, Jaycee. We all know how hard it's been. Yet you've kept going; you're one strong woman. Believe me, Cody will get over it. You made the right decision. Now it's time to move forward. Have you seen Sergei?"

"Not yet. He'll be going back to Russia soon, so…" There was a soft knock at the door.

"I'll get that, Jaycee. I told Jack I'd meet him downstairs. He must have gotten impatient and come up to get me."

"Okay, Megan. Thanks for your help." Jaycee went into the bathroom, closed the door and changed into her jeans and t-shirt. When she came back out, Megan was gone.

Sergei was standing in the middle of the room.

Jaycee's heart skipped a beat. "Sergei! What are you doing here?"

"Jaycee, why did you not tell me you were engaged to be married?" Sergei stepped forward and put his hands on her shoulders. "Listen to me. You cannot marry this man. I forbid it!"

Jaycee frowned. "Forbid? Who are you to tell me what to do, Sergei Volkov? I'll marry whomever I please!"

Sergei reached up and touched her cheek, his eyes now filled with tenderness, warmth and longing. "You cannot marry him because you must marry me, my *zvyozdochka*. I am going to stay in Canada and make a new life. Do you hear me? *Ya lyublyu tebya*. I love you, Jaycee McRae."

Jaycee looked at him in amazement, her eyes shining with hope. "You're staying? For good?"

Sergei drew her into his arms and kissed the top of her head. "I am staying. I will never leave you, Jaycee, and I will never stop loving you."

Jaycee wrapped her arms around his waist and rested her head on his chest. "I love you, too, Sergei. There is no engagement. I knew it was wrong and I ended it."

She looked up at him adoringly. "I had to do it because I love you, Sergei. I love you with all my heart."

Sergei took her face in his hands. His eyes were glistening with tears, but his smile shone with joy. "We will make a life together, my *zvyozdochka*. We will have many strong children and teach them to ride."

Without another word, Jaycee took his hand and led him to the bed.

CHAPTER 23

ownstairs, Jack Henderson waved to the waitress as Megan walked into the hotel café.

"Coffee?" he said as he got up and held out Megan's chair for her.

"Thanks, Jack." Megan sat, resting both arms on the table, one folded over the other.

As Jack took his seat, Megan smiled at him. "So, I just left Sergei with Jaycee. I think that might work out, despite your reservations about the Volkovs."

"About that…Megan, I have some things to tell you."

Jack explained everything to her, including why he had to warn Jaycee about the Volkovs while the investigation was still in progress. He told her about the takedown of Gagarin, and how the Volkovs had courageously helped to secure the arrest.

Megan gave a long low whistle. "Wow. You are a dark horse, Jack Henderson. I never thought I'd date an RCMP officer, much less one who takes down members of the Russian mafia. I don't know what to think!"

Jack smiled. "Think this. I want us to keep seeing each other, Megan. I thought I'd lost you for good last year, and I'm not prepared to lose you again. Would you consider moving to Calgary after the Stampede so we can be closer?"

Megan reached across the table and gripped his hand tightly. "Try and stop me, Detective Henderson!"

"And Jaycee? How is she?" Jack asked.

"Well, let me put it this way." Megan laughed. "I don't think I'll go back up to the room for a while. I think those two have some things to work out, if you know what I mean!"

"Megan, you are a wicked girl," Jack admonished.

"Don't I know it," said Megan with a smile.

CHAPTER 24

*T*he next afternoon, Jaycee rode into the arena with a new lease on life. She could see Sergei sitting with her parents in the grandstand. Megan and Jack were nearby. All of them were waving and smiling.

"Kerrie, this one is for you," Jaycee whispered and patted Luna on the neck. As she went through her routine, she felt a deep happiness and a renewed confidence.

Should she try the Drag just one more time? How could she not? Taking Luna into a gallop, she secured her right leg and began to drop backwards. She raised her left leg and pointed her toe.

Then she let go.

To her surprise, there was no fear. As she released her hands downward, she saw not a haunting vision of the past, but the smiling face of her beloved sister. It was as if, in that brief moment, Kerrie was reassuring her, urging her to move forward with her life.

Kerrie was fine. Jaycee knew that now. There was nothing to be afraid of.

She heard thunderous applause and the cheers of the crowd.

Jaycee swung back up into the saddle and waved, a triumphant smile on her face. The crowd was standing, giving her an ovation. She could see Sergei, her parents, Jack and Megan as they jumped to their feet, clapping madly.

Her heart surged with joy as she rode out of the arena.

EPILOGUE

"*L*ower your arm…that's right…a little lower…" Sergei called to his son. Five miles south of Okotoks, the Volkov family was rehearsing. It was a beautiful sunny day in late June.

"Sasha, watch your mother! See how she does it?" Twelve-year-old Sasha Volkov sat back down in the saddle, rode to the fence where his father was standing, and watched his mother execute a perfect Stroud Layout. A tall boy, he had his father's dark good looks and his mother's inner resolve and determination.

"We only have a week until the Stampede, my son," Sergei said. "Will you be ready?"

"*Da*, Papa. *Dedushka* has been helping me," Sasha answered.

Jaycee cantered up on her new horse, Bibi. "Did you see, sweetie?"

"Yes, Mama. I will try again." Sasha turned Luna back into the paddock and urged her into a gallop.

Ellis McRae and Petr Volkov walked out of the barn and joined Sergei and Jaycee as they watched their son.

"You see? The boy is doing well! That is because he listens to his *Dedushka*," Petr said, pointing to himself and grinning.

"What about his Pops?" Ellis said. "You're not the only grandpa around here, Petr!"

"He listens to both of you more than he listens to me," Sergei complained.

"Or me." Jaycee laughed. "You Volkov men!" she said, hopping off Bibi and leading her toward the barn. "You're so competitive! Come on into the house and let's see who can eat the most sandwiches at lunch!"

Ruth McRae was in the kitchen buttering bread for sandwiches as Jaycee came in and washed her hands in the back porch sink. Dmitri and Mikhail were having an arm wrestle over the kitchen table, grunting loudly.

"Yaaah!" Dmitri yelled as he slammed Mikhail's arm down. "Who is the strongest now?"

Mikhail grinned. "Not bad for a baby brother," he joked. "Of course, I let you win, so you wouldn't cry!" Dmitri responded by cuffing his brother playfully across the head.

"Enough, you two," said Sergei as he came in and sat at the table. "Time for lunch. Go wash!" Jaycee wrapped her arms around Sergei's neck and put her cheek against his.

"And what about you? Don't you need to wash?" Jaycee asked.

Sergei kissed her cheek. "I will, just let me enjoy my wife for a minute." He turned in his chair and drew her down onto his lap. "Ruth, am I not the luckiest man alive?" he asked his mother-in-law.

Ruth chuckled, putting a dish of potato salad on the table. "You are, son, you are! Now let her go so she can help me serve lunch."

Ellis and Petr arrived, discussing the building of a new barn on Petr's property next door, where he lived with his younger sons. They washed up and took their seats.

Sasha came running in just as lunch was being set on the table. He grabbed a sandwich and began stuffing it in his mouth.

"Sasha!" his grandmother scolded. Sasha sheepishly put the half-eaten sandwich on his plate and headed for the sink.

Finally, the whole family was at the table.

"Let's give thanks," said Ruth. Everyone joined hands as Ellis prayed.

"Now, we eat!" Petr exclaimed. "*Da*, Sasha?"

"*Za zdorov'ye!*" said Sasha. And they all laughed.

The End

～

Love the novel you just read?
Your opinion matters.

Review this book on your favorite book site, review site, blog, or your own social media properties, and share your opinion with other readers.

Thank you for taking the time to write a review for me!

WOMEN OF STAMPEDE SERIES

Saddle up for the ride! The Women of Stampede will lasso your hearts! If you love romance novels with a western flair, look no further than the Women of Stampede Series. Authors from Calgary, Red Deer, Edmonton and other parts of the province have teamed up to create seven contemporary romance novels loosely themed around The Greatest Outdoor Show on Earth... the Calgary Stampede. Among our heroes and heroines, you'll fall in love with innkeepers, country singers, rodeo stars, barrel racers, chuckwagon drivers, trick riders, Russian Cossack riders, western-wear designers and bareback riders. And we can't forget our oil executives, corporate planners, mechanics, nursing students and executive chefs. We have broken hearts, broken bodies, and broken spirits to mend, along with downed fences and shattered relationships. Big city lights. Small town nights. And a fabulous blend of city dwellers and country folk for your reading pleasure. Best of all, hearts are swelling with love, looking for Mr. or Miss Right and a happily ever after ending. Seven fabulous books from seven fabulous authors featuring a loosely connected theme—The Calgary Stampede.

WOMEN OF STAMPEDE BOOKS

Hearts in the Spotlight, Katie O'Connor
The Half Mile of Baby Blue, Shelley Kassian
Saddle a Dream, Brenda Sinclair
Eden's Charm, C.G. Furst
Unbridled Steele, Nicole Roy
Betting on Second Chances, Alyssa Linn Palmer
Trick of the Heart, Maeve Buchanan

ABOUT MAEVE BUCHANAN

Maeve Buchanan grew up on the Canadian prairies in a family of avid readers. She spent much of her childhood perusing fictional worlds, and soon began imagining her own fictional stories.

Maeve has a degree in English Literature and Medieval Studies and has been employed at a wide variety of interesting jobs, including graphic arts, building playgrounds in the Arctic, working as an historical interpreter, teaching medieval literature and marketing for a major bookstore chain.

After joining the Romance Writers of America (Calgary chapter), Maeve's literary talents found a new home in the Romance genre. Maeve's current work, Trick of the Heart, is an adult contemporary Western romance set during the spectacular Calgary Exhibition and Stampede. She currently resides in Edmonton, Alberta, Canada.

Visit her website at: https://www.maevebuchanan.com/
Follow her on Social media:

facebook.com/maevebuchananauthor

twitter.com/MaeveBuchanan77

amazon.com/author/Maeve-Buchanan

CPSIA information can be obtained
at www.ICGtesting.com
Printed in the USA
LVOW11s2228040518
575778LV00001BA/6/P